BEYOND THE
BEANSTALK

BEYOND THE
BEANSTALK

KAYE UMANSKY

ILLUSTRATED BY CHRIS FISHER

Hodder
Children's
Books

a division of Hodder Headline plc

Text copyright © 1997 by Kaye Umansky
Illustrations copyright © 1997 by Chris Fisher

First published in Great Britain in 1997
by Hodder Children's Books

The right of Kaye Umansky and Chris Fisher to be identified as
the Author and Illustrator of the Work has been asserted by
them in accordance with the Copyright, Designs and Patents Act
1988.

10   9   8   7   6   5   4   3   2   1

A Catalogue record for this book is available from the
British Library.

ISBN 0 340 67306 0

Printed and bound in Great Britain by
Mackays of Chatham PLC, Chatham, Kent

Hodder Children's Books
A Division of Hodder Headline plc
338 Euston Road
London NW1 3BH

CONTENTS

1	The Row	7
2	The Lane	15
3	The Witch	22
4	The Homecoming	35
5	The Beanstalk	49
6	The Climb	58
7	The Giantess	64
8	The Relations	77
9	The Discovery	89
10	The Journey	96
11	The Princess	101
12	The Accident	114
13	The Mousehole	122
14	The Plan	130
15	The Descent	139
16	The Kitchen	146
17	The Cat	156
18	The Escape	166
19	The Parting	174
20	The Happy Ending	186

For Ella

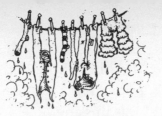

CHAPTER ONE

THE ROW

In which Our Hero gets an earful

"You know, I've been thinking," said Jack's ma.

Uh-oh, thought Jack. Here we go. Whatever happens, say nothing.

It was a rainy Monday. He was sitting in the steamy kitchen with the cat on his lap, feet up on the ironing board, minding his own business, generally taking it easy. His ma was standing at the steaming washtub, grimly thumping away with a stout stick. Lines of wet clothes hung about the place, dripping into buckets.

"I've been wondering which is worse," went on his ma. "Being poor, then rich, then poor again, or never having been rich in the first place."

Thump, thump, thump! went the stick.

Say nothing, thought Jack.

"I think, on the whole, I'd sooner have just stayed poor. Then at least I wouldn't know what I was missing."

Thump, thump, thump!

Say nothing, thought Jack.

"My beautiful furniture, my jewels, my gowns, my lovely palace, gone, all gone. And it's all *your* fault - starting with the cow."

Not the cow, thought Jack. Anything but the cow.

"'Make sure you get a decent price for her,' I said. 'Mind you don't get diddled.' Those were my very words. And what do you do? Exchange her for a handful of magic beans! Hah! You should have stayed home and helped your mother, instead of cavorting off up beanstalks. Bringing home all that magic rubbish."

She snatched a steaming kettle from the stove and poured more boiling water into the tub. Clouds of fresh steam billowed angrily around the kitchen

"Wasn't rubbish," Jack mumbled. He couldn't help it. It just fell out of his mouth.

"What did you say? Did you speak?"

"I'm just *saying*." He had done it now.

8

"I'm just *saying*. It wasn't all rubbish, Ma. I didn't see you turning your nose up at all that gold, for a start."

"Don't you be so cheeky! Anyway, gold goes nowhere these days. Palaces take a lot of upkeep. The gold-plated toilet cost an arm and a leg for starters."

Angrily, she started threading a wet vest through the mangle. The way she was turning the handle, Jack had a feeling she wished it was him going through.

"We didn't *have* to get a palace," he pointed out reasonably. "We could have got a bigger cottage. One with a bit of head height. One where I wouldn't brain myself every time I walk out the door."

"So you'd deny your mother a palace, would you?" cried his ma bitterly, hands on hips.

"No, no! It's just . . . well. A gold plated toilet! I mean! Was it *really* necessary?"

"Yes! What do you know about interior decoration? What makes me so cross is, we'd still be there now, living in the lap of luxury, if you hadn't let the hen get out. Deny that, if you can!"

Jack opened his mouth, then closed it again. There was no arguing with that. It was true. They had only been living in the palace a matter of months when, one never to be forgotten night, he had carelessly left open the door to the chicken coop. The following morning, it was empty. The precious, golden egg-laying hen had wandered out, over the hills and far away, where the sun shone, the worms were juicy and your eggs were your own to do what you liked with.

What a row that had caused. No more golden eggs. No more wild spending sprees. The bailiffs had moved in, the palace had been sold, and it was next stop: humble cottage. Again.

"I think I'll go to my room for a bit," said Jack, putting down the cat and edging his way through the steam towards the ladder leading up to the loft where he slept. "Work on the Magic Harp, you know?"

"You'll do no such thing!" snapped his ma. "You'll stay here and fold the ironing. I'm bothered if I'm slaving over a hot tub while you sit about fiddling with that stupid harp all day."

"You don't fiddle with a harp," said Jack, in a hopeful attempt at hearty humour. "You fiddle with a violin. Ta-da!"

It was only a little joke. Life was short of a few laughs these days. Of course, it fell flatter than a cement pancake.

"Don't you be clever with me! Anyway, all the fiddling in the world's not going to fix that harp. It's *broken*. You put your great, clumsy foot through it when you came down off the beanstalk."

"Well, there was a giant coming down after me at the time . . ."

"There you go again! Argue, argue, always argue. And mind how you fold that shirt! That's Lord Bellicose's shirt, that is, and he's fussy. Oh, to think that a short while ago all the toffs in the land were begging for an invitation to one of my palace balls and now I'm washing their underwear! From balls to smalls in six months! Ah me!"

And she burst into tears. A big one rolled down to the end of her nose and fell into the washtub with a sad little plop.

"There, there," muttered Jack, patting her shoulder awkwardly. "Don't take on so."

"I hate being a washerwoman!" howled his ma. "I'm used to better things!"

"I know, I know. But you've still got me."

"Yes, more's the pity. Oh, give me that shirt, you'll never do it right!"

Crossly, she snatched it away. Jack watched her thumping the sleeves into place and sighed. Poverty didn't suit her, that was for sure. It made her pinched and shrewish.

Mind you, she hadn't made too good a job of being rich either. She was probably the only woman in the entire kingdom who found it hard to manage on one solid gold egg a day.

"What's for tea?" asked Jack, hoping to change the subject.

"Nothing. We're down to the last barley cake. I'm saving that for our breakfast tomorrow. Of course, if you'd get a job it would help."

"I've tried," said Jack wearily. They had been this way before. "I keep telling you. There's not a lot of call for a giant killer. There's been a giant shortage."

"Something else, then. Odd jobs. Gardening or something."

"I'm hopeless at gardening. You know that. Snails follow me round. I'm their Pied Piper."

"Oh, I can't be bothered to argue with you!" cried his ma. She picked up a bag of washing and thrust it at him. "Here. Make yourself useful for once. Take this along to Old Mother Skinnard. It's her winter vests. And make sure she doesn't cheat you. She doesn't like parting with her money, that one. She'll pretend she can't find her purse and try and palm you off with a handful of maggoty old carrots or suchlike. Three pennies I want, and don't you come back without them. Go on."

Jack shouldered the bag. From Killer Of Giants to Deliverer Of Vests was a bit of a come down in the world - but right now, anything would do to get him out of the place.

As he usually did when leaving the humble cottage, he cracked his head painfully upon the low beam.

"Watch out for the beam!" cried his ma - too late, as always.

CHAPTER TWO

THE LANE

In which Our Hero reflects on past glories

Outside, it was drizzling and the snails were out in force as usual. Huge great gangs of them, slowly but relentlessly munching up the garden.

They ate everything, those snails. All Jack's pathetic attempts at growing vegetables had been foiled by them. Lettuces, beans, radishes - they chomped their way through the lot, leaving silvery slime trails in their wake.

"Gerroff!" he growled. They waved their eye stalks at him and deliberately carried on eating. *Go on,* they seemed to be saying. *Plant another row of lettuces and see how you get on, mate.*

Disgustedly, Jack picked his way between them and kicked the gate shut behind him.

Thunder grumbled in the distance as he set off down the lane. It looked like another downpour was in the offing. And him in his shirt sleeves with no jerkin, no cap, and holes in his boots.

Sighing, he hefted the bag of washing to his other shoulder. What a way to spend a wet Monday!

There was nothing worse than being a failed hero.

Being a successful, hero, now - that was something else altogether. He cast his mind back to those heady days, just after he had killed the giant. Things had been all right then. People had treated him with respect. There had been a celebration feast on the village green, he remembered, with roast ox and jolly paper hats and a big *Welcome Home* cake with proper icing and cherries on the top. The Mayor had made a flattering speech along the lines of *Local Boy Makes Good*. Cheering villagers had queued up to touch his famous axe and thank him, with tears in their eyes, for putting Lower Muckheap on the map.

The local children had learned a new folk

dance in his honour. It was called *The Killer*, and featured the symbolic hacking down of the maypole.

A minstrel had composed a special song for the occasion. The catchy chorus went "Down 'e come with a bing, bang, boom!" It was on people's lips for weeks.

But all that was before the worst thing imaginable happened.

The giant began to smell!

As ill luck would have it, it had been a particularly hot summer that year. Far from being a tourist attraction, as the Mayor had hoped, the mouldering ogre very quickly became a public nuisance. Great, buzzing armies of immigrant flies arrived and set up home in his beard. There was a run on pot pourri at the village shop and, when the wind was in the east, everyone took to sleeping with the windows closed.

Eventually, after several emergency meetings in the village hall, during which phrases like "outrage" and "public disgrace" and "Jack's fault" were bandied about a bit, the desperate villagers had put clothes pegs on their noses, harnessed up their horses, hauled the giant up to the downs and buried him in a deep hole which had turned out to be not quite deep enough. Even now, you could see where his tummy poked up. The village children sledged down it in the winter.

Jack had kept a low profile during this stage of the operation. He and his ma had recently moved into the palace, paid for in golden eggs. The palace was on top of a hill, far enough from the village so that the smell of rotting giant wasn't a problem. When Jack heard of the Giant Disposal Plan, he had wanted to help - but his ma put her foot down, saying that it wasn't the Done Thing, now he was a hero and living in a palace; that he'd ruin his lovely new suit and that there were poor people to do nasty jobs like that.

That was a bad move. The villagers held strong views on Folks Who Were Hoity Toity. From then on, people cut Jack dead in the streets. Gangs of small children ran after him and jeered at his smart new clothes whenever he wandered down the hill to buy a newspaper. Old men stopped in the road and waved their sticks at him. Old ladies shook their feeble fists. Dogs growled at him. A rumour started that he hadn't even killed the giant! That the giant had got dizzy and fallen down by accident, and that Jack's sterling work with the axe had had nothing to do with it.

19

When, finally, the hen escaped and everything went wrong, ending with Jack and his ma being evicted from the palace and moving back into the humble cottage, you could sense the villagers' glee. It was amazing what short memories people had . . .

His bitter reflections were interrupted by the sight of three village women standing chatting in the lane ahead: Mrs Dumpkins, Dame Pimble and the Widow McBride. They nudged each other when they saw him coming.

"Morning, Jack," said Mrs Dumpkins, who considered herself a bit of a wit. "Out looking for the famous missing hen, are we? Hopin' to find a pile of *chicken nuggets* layin' about in the hedge or somethin? Nuggets. Get it?"

Dame Pimble and the Widow McBride tittered behind their hands.

"No, actually," said Jack politely. "I'm delivering some washing for Ma."

"Well, there! An' I thought you was hen huntin'. I knew you couldn't be out lookin' fer giants, cos you aint got yer axe. Let's 'ope there aint one round the corner, eh? 'Course, you could always batter 'im round the 'ead with a wet vest."

More sniggers. Jack gave a tired, tight smile and trudged on. The three women watched him go.

"He's got his comeuppance all right," said Mrs Dumpkins, with a self-satisfied sniff.

"That's right," agreed the Widow McBride. "Him and his hoity toity ma."

"Serves 'em right," nodded Mrs Pimble.

Jack rounded the corner and allowed himself an almighty kick at a stone in the road, just to let off steam. It hurt his foot, of course, as you might expect. Then he climbed over a five barred gate, dropped into a muddy puddle and squelched off miserably across the open fields towards the dripping woods in the distance.

That's when the clouds *really* opened.

CHAPTER THREE

THE WITCH

In which Our Hero gets into a soup

"Yes?" squawked a shrill voice from behind the door of a tumbledown hovel. "Ooozat?"

"It's only me, Mrs Skinnard. Jack. Come with your vests."

"I aint ordered no chests."

"It's Jack!" bellowed Jack. "Jack the Giant Killer! Ma sent me with the washing! Come on, it's chucking it down out here!"

"Oh, Jack the *Giant Killer*. Why dint yer say so?"

There was the sound of grumbling, the rattle of a chain and the door opened. Two suspicious little eyes peered out at him from a tangle of mad grey hair, like blackberries in a thicket.

"You'm soppin' wet," Old Mother Skinnard told him unecessarily. "You'd better come in." She narrowed her eyes and added darkly, "That's if you aint too frited. With all them dark roomers."

"Roomers?" said Jack, puzzled. What, did she take in lodgers or something?

"You know." Old Mother Skinnard lowered her voice to a thrilling hiss and nudged him in the ribs with a sharp elbow. "*You* know. About me bein' a witch an' that. Scarin' all the kiddies. Dancin' widdershins in the moonlight. Puttin' curses on folk. You know. Roomers. You must 'ave 'eard 'em."

She peered at him hopefully.

"I haven't heard any rumours," said Jack.

Well, he hadn't. He never heard any of the local gossip these days, because nobody talked to him.

"No?" Old Mother Skinnard sounded a bit miffed. "I must say I'm surprised. Very suprised indeed. Oh well. Come in, if you'm comin'. An shut the door be'ind you. I don't want Crabbit gettin' out."

Shaking off the rain, Jack stepped in and stared around.

It was all pretty much as he had expected. Cobwebs, shadows, broomstick propped in corner, sagging shelves containing rows and rows of dusty jars, bunches of mysterious herbs, the inevitable piles of yellowing old newspapers . . . standard Mad Witch. There was even a bubbling cauldron set over the fire. As an extra touch, the floor was white with bird droppings: courtesy of a large, black crow which crouched in the shadows on a rafter overhead. Crabbit, presumably.

"Crabbit, Jack; Jack, Crabbit," said Old Mother Skinnard.

"Who's a pretty boy, then?" said Jack conversationally, stopping beneath the rafter and wiggling his finger.

"Don't patronise *me*, sonny," rasped the crow, and pointedly turned its back.

"Ignore 'im," advised Old Mother Skinnard. "'E's a miserable old so-and-so. We 'ad words this mornin'. I told 'im off fer not pullin' 'is weight an' 'elpin' me with me mystic rites. I'm thinkin' of swappin' 'im fer a toad. At least you don't get the back-chat. So. Wacha think o' the place?"

She peered hopefully up at him through her wild bush of hair, obviously fishing for compliments. "Lovely," said Jack. "The - er - broomstick's a nice touch."

The Witch

Actually, he felt she'd overdone it - but it was best to humour the daft old thing.

"It flies, you know," Old Mother Skinnard told him. "It aint just fer show, if that's what you'm thinkin'."

"Oh, I wasn't," lied Jack.

"Yes you was. You'm just like the others." Old Mother Skinnard gave a disgusted little sniff. "You thinks I'm just another crazy ole woman what makes things up. You don't really think I'm a witch at all, do yer?"

"Oh, I do, I do," Jack hastened to reassure her, privately thinking that of all the crazy old women he'd ever met, this one took the cake. "Really. I bet you cackle away under the moon like billyo."

Old Mother Skinnard gave him a funny look, snatched the bag of washing, dumped it on the table and began poking through.

"I 'ope yer ma's used the right soap this time," she remarked sourly. "Brings me out in a rash, that cheap stuff. 'Ow much do I owe?"

"Three pennies."

"Daylight robbery! I suppose she thinks she's still up at the palace, queenin' it around with the nobs. You'm not tellin' me she's short of a few bob."

"I wish," said Jack, with a little sigh.

"Garn! I'll wager she's got plenty stashed away. What 'appened to all them glitzy jewels? And them fancy frocks she went poncin' about in?"

"Sold. Went to pay off the debts."

"What about yer axe, then? That there famous axe what did fer the giant? There's people'd pay a pretty penny fer that."

"Sadly, no," said Jack, a little stiffly. "We tried putting it up for auction, but there weren't any takers. When it came to digging in their pockets, people seemed to forget its glorious history. As a matter of fact, it's at home rusting in the woodshed. Look, I don't want to rush you, but . . . ?"

"All in good time, all in good time. Talkin' of axes reminds me. I gotta few logs need splittin' up. Strong lad like you, shouldn't take more'n a few minutes. Over by the fireplace. Chopper's on the hook."

Jack looked. There were considerably more than a few. Half the forest was lying there, waiting to be whittled down to size. Old Mother Skinnard saw the look on his face.

"You wouldn't be about to refuse, now, would you?" she said. "'Cos I'm tellin' you now. I got ways of makin' you work. One little wave of me wand, that's all it takes, an' I got you in me power. You'll be choppin' logs an' carryin' water an' muckin' out me drains from 'ere to eternity. I can do it, you know."

"That won't be necessary," said Jack, remembering his manners. "I'd be glad to help out, Mrs Skinnard. I wouldn't want you to waste your - ahem - mystic skills on me."

"There's a good lad!" beamed Old Mother Skinnard approvingly. "You get crackin' an' I'll see if I can lay me 'ands on me purse."

Stifling a sigh, Jack walked over to the woodpile and hefted the chopper. For a long while, nothing could be heard but the rhythmic sound of chopping, interspersed with squealing drawers and slamming cupboard doors as Old Mother Skinnard rummaged.

Getting through the woodpile took even longer than Jack thought. Just when he reckoned he was down to the last log, another one always seemed to turn up. To make things worse, the crow was smirking at him

from the rafters and making sneering noises deep in its throat. It was most off-putting.

"I can't find it," declared Old Mother Skinnard, coming up from behind and making him jump. "You'll 'ave to wait till next month. I got some nice carrots, though, if you . . . ?"

"Sorry," said Jack, firmly. He set down the chopper. "I've got to have the money, Mrs Skinnard. We need it for bread. Ma was very definite. She'll kill me if I come home with carrots."

Old Mother Skinnard's beady little eyes flickered up and down him, taking in his shabby breeches and worn-out boots.

"Things that bad, eh? Still no news of the missing hen, I suppose?"

"No."

"And that Magic Harp you bust? Still tryin' ter fix it?"

"Yes, if you must know," said Jack shortly.

Both hen and harp were sore points.

"You'm wastin' yer time there," Old Mother Skinnard told him flatly. "You aint got the know-'ow. Takes skill to fix a magic instrument."

"I know," said Jack bitterly. "I know I'm hopeless." Then he added, with a sudden rush of anger, "But I wasn't always, I'll have you know! I've had my moments. Up there, I mean. Up the beanstalk. I was somebody to be reckoned with up there. I was fast. And crafty. And brave, yes, brave! But everyone seems to forget that."

"All right, all right. Keep yer 'air on," said Old Mother Skinnard. "Only makin' conversation."

There was a pause. Jack felt a bit embarrassed by his outburst.

"Sorry," he mumbled. "It's just that it gets to me sometimes."

"Ah, forget it," said Old Mother Skinnard cheerfully. "We all 'as our off days. Even when we'm meant to be livin' 'appily ever after. Fancy a drop o' turnip soup?"

"Well . . ."

"Go on. It's nice. It's not often I 'as company."

Jack considered. The offer of a free meal wasn't one to be turned down lightly.

"Well - all right, then. I am a bit peckish. Thanks."

He sat carefully on the edge of a white splattered chair while Old Mother Skinnard busied herself at the cauldron.

"There you go," she said, placing a steaming bowl before him. It smelled good. Cautiously, he raised it to his lips, blew and sipped.

"All right, is it?"

"Mmmm. Lovely."

It was, too. There was a pause while he ravenously tucked in. Old Mother Skinnard stood watching him with an inscrutable expression on her face. Her skinny arms were folded across her chest and her head was on one side, like a bird. Then, suddenly, quite out of the blue, she said:

"Fancy another crack at it, then?"

"Sorry? Another crack at what?"

"What d'you think? The beanstalk."

"Look," said Jack. "I really don't think there's any point . . ."

"Well, do yer or don't yer?" cried Old Mother Skinnard. "If you 'ad the chance, would you go up there again? That's what I'm gettin' at."

"Well - yes, of course, but . . ."

"Right. And what would you do once you got up there, might I ask?"

Jack thought. What would he do?

"Well," he said slowly. "Well, there's the treasure, for a start. We're desperately poor, you know, and you've got to be practical. A bag or two of gold would come in handy. I know some people might say it's stealing, but what they forget is that it never belonged to the giants in the first place. It was all pinched from titchies."

"Titchies?"

"That's what the giants call us. There's no *big* treasure up there. It's all human-sized. It stands to reason they stole it. So, yes, I'd definitely help myself to more gold. But actually . . ."

He trailed off, aware that what he was about to say might sound a bit hypocritical.

"Actually what?" urged Old Mother Skinnard. "Go on. Say it."

"Actually, what I'd really like to do is call in on the giant's wife. She was very kind to me, you know. Made me bacon sandwiches."

32

"Giant's *widow,* you mean," Old Mother Skinnard reminded him. "You did for 'er 'ubby, remember?"

Jack flushed. It was true, of course. He didn't need reminding. The memory still kept him awake at night.

"It was self-defence," he muttered uncomfortably. "Him or me. Anyway, he was a rotten husand. Bossed her around all the time. Wife, do this; wife, do that. And he was terrible company. Never really talked to her. *Fee Fi Fo Fum* was one of his *better* sentences."

"Still . . ." said Old Mother Skinnard, eyebrows raised quizzically.

"Yes, well, all right, I do feel badly, if you must know. But what's done is done. I had my chance and I messed up all round. It's too late to put things right now."

"Hmmm," said Old Mother Skinnard. "You're wrong there, you know. Leastways, it's never too late to try."

She suddenly turned and scuttled across to the dresser shelves. She pulled out a small footstool, stood on it with her back to him and began running her fingers along the ranks of jars. Whatever she was looking for, it wasn't her purse.

Jack gave a sigh, swallowed the last of the soup and stood up. "I think I'd better be getting on now; Ma'll be wondering where I am . . ."

"Don't you want payin'?" enquired Old Mother Skinnard, climbing down off the footstool.

"Well - yes."

"Three, weren't it?"

"That's right," said Jack. Things were looking up.

"'Old out your mitt, then."

Jack did as he was told, and into his palm she placed . . . three beans.

"What're these?" said Jack, staring down at them.

"Magic Beans," said Old Mother Skinnard, with the triumphant air of a conjuror. "Told you I was a witch, didn't I?"

CHAPTER FOUR

THE HOMECOMING

In which Our Hero goes home with more than he bargained for

Outside, darkness was falling, along with the rain.

"'Bye, then," said Old Mother Skinnard. "Mind how you go."

"Look," said Jack desperately, "look, don't you understand? I can't take these . . ."

"Course you can. Think of 'em as payment fer choppin' me kindlin'. You'm a good lad at 'eart. You deserves another chance. Everyone does."

"But . . ."

"Go on. Off with you. Oh - before I fergets . . ."

She reached into her rags, drew out a crumpled paper bag and thrust it into his hand. "Emergency kit. Just a few bits 'an bobs that might 'elp you, if you gets into trouble. Nothin' much. Just an Extra Strength Pill an' a little bottle o' Love Potion an' a pair o' Seven League Socks ter give you an extra burst o'speed. You can only use everythin' the once, mind, so don't go wastin' 'em. You gotta be sensible with magic stuff. You gotta use it at the proper time an' place."

"But . . ."

"Now listen, sonny." Old Mother Skinnard's voice had developed a sharp edge. She had had enough of standing in the doorway in the freezing rain. She waved a finger at Jack. "I knows what you'm thinkin'. You'm thinkin' I'm tryin' ter pull a fast one. But you'm wrong. Them beans is genuine. I knows me stuff when it comes to Magic Beans. D'you think silly old codgers you meets in lanes 'as got a monopoly on Magic Beans or summint? A bit of gratitude wouldn't come amiss, specially now I've thrown in all them extras, but I s'pose that's youth today. Now, off you go, before I changes me mind."

And she slammed the door in his face.

Jack couldn't believe it. He stood there under the dripping trees, clutching the paper bag and the three beans. Whatever would his ma say? Despite her warnings, he had let himself be diddled yet again. Whatever was the matter with him? Why was he such a pushover?

Heart once again in his boots (where it seemed to spend a lot of time these days) he thrust the bag deep in his pocket and turned to leave.

Just then, there came the sound of raised voices. One belonged to Old Mother Skinnard. The other had a familiar, rasping quality. Suddenly, the door shot open again. There was a flapping noise, a squawk, and something shot out in a flurry of feathers and landed in a muddy puddle at his feet. The door banged shut again with a final kind of sound.

It was the crow. He shook the mud off his feathers, stared up at Jack with beady little eyes and snapped: "What you starin' at? Never seen a bird take a mud bath before?"

"Oh, is *that* what you're doing?" said Jack. "And there was me thinking you've just been kicked out. Funny, that."

"Yes, go on, be a clever dick, why don't you? It's bad enough that you've gone and upset her. And who does she take it out on? Me. I suppose that makes you really happy."

"Actually, I couldn't care less," said Jack, with a shrug. "I've got enough troubles of my own."

He turned his back and began to walk away.

"Hold it!"

There was a flurry of wings, and suddenly sharp talons dug into his shoulder and feathers tickled his ear.

"What d'you think you're doing?" objected Jack. His neck nearly walked off his shoulders in an effort to get his head away.

"What does it look like? I'm comin' with you."

"No chance," said Jack. "Get off my shoulder. I've seen what you did to the floor."

"Nope. I've got my orders." The crow waved a claw at the firmly closed hovel door. "*She* says I've gotta keep an eye on you. It's you an' me, son."

"Look," said Jack, tightly. "Look, Crabby, or whatever your name is—"

"Crabbit."

"Right. Well, Crabbit, let's put it this way.

I've just been cheated out of three pennies and palmed off with a load of old junk. I appreciate your offer, but to be quite honest, a crow with an attitude is the last thing I need right now."

"What d'you mean? What 'ave I done?" enquired Crabbit, in an aggrieved sort of way.

"You sneered at me. When I was chopping the logs. You made mocking noises in your throat."

"So? I was crowing. I'm a crow. What do you expect?"

"I expect you to eat snails or build a nest in a tree or whatever it is crows do. I don't expect you to stand around arguing the toss with me. If you want to know the truth, I don't like talking birds. I've *never* liked talking birds. They're unnatural. Now, kindly get off my shoulder before I do something we'll both regret."

He raised his hand threateningly. There was a whoosh, a lightening sensation in the shoulder area, and Crabbit was suddenly peering down at him from the branch of a nearby tree.

"No need for that kind of talk," he muttered sulkily. "Anyway, what you making such a fuss about a few pennies for? You got Magic Beans."

"Magic!" sneered Jack. "Hah!"

He opened his hand and curled his lip contemptously at the small brown objects that lay there. He bunched his fist, and drew back his arm, ready to hurl them away in disgust.

"That's right," jeered Crabbit. "Go on. Chuck 'em away without even tryin' 'em out. Act like a mug. You're good at that, by all accounts."

"Ah - button your beak," growled Jack. But he didn't throw the beans away. Instead, he thrust them into his pocket. Then, without a backward glance, he turned on his heel and trudged off into the dark trees.

Crabbit watched until he was out of sight, then took off with a harsh cry, skimming low over the tree-tops, rain glinting on his sleek black feathers.

"Have you seen the time? Past ten o'clock!" cried Jack's ma as he entered, cracking his head on the low beam as usual. "Where've you been?"

"Ouch! Nowhere. I stopped for a chat with Old Mother Skinnard. Chopped up a bit of kindling for her."

"There're plenty of jobs doing around here if you're looking for work. Look at you, dripping all over my floor. Where's the money?"

"Ah. Well, you see, Ma, there was a bit of a problem. She couldn't find her purse. But she did give me a nice bowl of soup and . . ."

He ducked as the scrubbing board sailed over his head, missing him by a hair's breadth.

"S O U P ?" howled his ma, setting about him with her s c r u b b i n g brush. "I'll give you soup, you great (*whack!*) - stupid (*whack!*) - no good (*whack!*) - idiot! " (*Whack, whack, WHACK!*)

"Ow! Hold on, no need to - ow! Mind my - OW!"

Arms shielding his head, Jack made a dash for the ladder. Bars of hard, yellow soap rained around him as he scrambled up.

"You wait!" screeched his ma. "You wait till you come down out of there! I'll give you soup, my lad!"

With a little moan, he fell into his room, slammed the door shut and dropped the bar. It was made of good, stout wood. Mercifully, her wails became muffled.

Pausing only to light the single candle

stub that was stuck in a niche on the wall, Jack picked his way carefully between the bits of dismembered harp littering the floor. Thankfully, he collapsed on his narrow bed, closed his eyes and let out a long, quivering breath of relief. Peace at last. It had been a long, long day.

And then: *Tap, tap, tap!*

There came an urgent tapping on the streaming window pane. Unwillingly, Jack forced one eye open.

Tap, tap, tap, TAP!

There it was again! With a sigh, Jack struggled upright, trudged to the window and threw it open. A gust of rain blew in his face.

"You again," he said, wearily.

"Yep." Crabbit was crouched on the outer ledge, looking bedraggled and tetchy. "You don't get rid of me that easily, son. Let me in, then. I've been waiting for ages."

"How come? I've only just got back," remarked Jack, stepping to one side (although much against his better judgement). The bird hopped in, leaving a trail of single wet claw marks on the window sill.

"Ah, but look at the silly *route* you took. All

those twists an' turns an' climbin' gates an' followin' windin' lanes an' rubbish. I came straight. As the crow flies, you know?"

His beady black eyes flickered around Jack's shabby little room, taking in the threadbare rug, the chipped wash jug and the worn jerkin hanging from a rusty nail.

"So. This is how the giant killing classes live. Lovely!" he remarked, then fluttered from the sill onto the bed rail and began to preen his feathers.

"Make yourself at home, why don't you?" said Jack, sarcastically.

"Thanks. I will."

Jack suddenly found that he was too tired to argue any more. He turned his back on the unwelcome visitor and began to unlace his sodden boots. Yawning, he kicked them off, eased off his wet socks, removed his saturated shirt, dropped it on the floor and pulled on his old, faded nightshirt.

Before removing his breeches, he suddenly remembered Old Mother Skinnard's final offering. He reached into the pocket and pulled out the crumpled paper bag.

"What's this old rubbish?" he growled.

He sat on the edge of the bed and inspected the items, one by one. It was a disappointing collection.

There was a small orange pill, which looked worryingly like the one the cat had for furballs. It was vaguely fluffy, as though it had been hanging around for some time.

There was a tiny, corked bottle containing a quantity of unpleasant looking dark brown liquid. He pulled out the cork and sniffed it cautiously. It didn't smell at all magical. In fact, it smelled of liquorice.

Lastly, there were two well worn, faded blue, woolly socks rolled into a ball. They looked like rejects from a jumble sale. When Jack unrolled them, he found that one had a hole in the heel.

Disgustedly, he thrust the uninspiring gifts back into the bag.

"Extra Strength Pill," he muttered. "Love Potion. Seven League Socks. Hah!"

"You've got the beans safe, I hope?" enquired Crabbit, pausing in his preening.

"Yes," said Jack. "Not that it's any of your business."

"I should plant 'em, then. Sooner the better, if you want my advice."

"I don't."

Nevertheless, he reached into his left pocket and brought out the beans, inspecting them closely by the light of the candle. He was looking for some sign that they were special, out of the ordinary beans. Perhaps some minute carvings, or a subtle change of colouration.

But no. They were just beans. They didn't make your palm tingle, or possess some deep, mysterious inner glow. Just beans.

Still . . .

"Get a move on, then," prompted Crabbit, sounding peevish. "Don't take all night. It's past my perch time."

"I'm doing it, I'm doing it, all right?"

With a sigh, Jack clambered to his feet and once again moved to the window.

Crabbit watched, head on one side and black eyes gleaming.

Rather to Jack's surprise, he found that the rain had stopped. A pale, watery moon slid in and out of clouds, bathing the weed-ridden, snail-infested garden in silver.

Feeling rather silly, he leaned out, swallowed hard, crossed his fingers for luck and threw the beans out. They landed in the soft, wet soil below.

"Attaboy!" said Crabbit. And without another word, he stuck his head under his wing and, rather ostentatiously, began to snore.

Shivering a little, Jack closed the window, uncrossed his fingers and groped his way back to bed; although not before stepping heavily on the fiddly little triangular bit of harp which never seemed to fit right.

That was that, then. It would *never* fit now.

Muttering under his breath, he picked up the piece of buckled metal and hurled it into a corner. Then, finally, he crawled into his cold bed, and, within seconds, was asleep.

Down below, in the kitchen, his ma sat weeping into a cup of tea and eating the last barley cake while the cat dribbled on Lord Bellicose's neatly ironed shirts.

And outside, storm-watered and caressed by the moon, the beanstalk began to grow.

CHAPTER FIVE

THE BEANSTALK

In which things begin to look up for Our Hero

When Jack went down to breakfast the following morning, he found his grey-faced ma staring hollow-eyed at the kitchen window, holding on to the table for support. She was still in her dressing gown and curlers. For once, the place wasn't full of steam. The kettles were cold, the wash-tub was empty and the room was filled with a strange, luminous green light.

The cat, sitting by its empty plate, went rigid at Jack's entrance, and growled deep in its throat. Its eyes were fixed on Jack's shoulder.

"Oh, Jack," said his ma in a trembling voice, not even looking at him. "It's happened again, son."

"I know," said Jack. He went over and gave her hand a comforting little pat. "Take it easy, Ma. I'm finding it hard to believe, myself."

He followed her gaze to the window. Great, green leaves pressed darkly against the leaded pane, blocking out the sun. Here and there, clusters of long pods hung from the branches like limp fingers. It was as though the jungle had marched all the way from distant parts and was now clamouring to get in and put its roots up.

Behind them, the cat crept forward, inch by inch, tail flicking and glitter-

ing eyes still fixed on Jack's shoulder.

"But how?" wailed his ma. "How did it hap—" She broke off with a little scream. "What's *that* on your shoulder?"

"Oh, you mean *this*?" said Jack, acting casual. "Oh, this is just a spare crow Old Mother Skinnard had lying around. It's called Crabbit. It - er - talks, I'm afraid."

"Please!" objected Crabbit, sounding highly offended. "Give me some credit. I don't just *talk*, son. I converse. I discuss. I debate. We're not talkin' budgie here. And will somebody get that flamin' cat out?"

Jack's ma clutched a chair back to keep herself from falling. The cat, unused to conversation from its intended breakfast, gave a hiss and bolted from the room with its hair on end. Crabbit looked smug.

"Ignore him," advised Jack. "Now, listen, Ma, because this is important. Old Mother Skinnard gave me some more Magic Beans. I know, I know, you warned me not to get fobbed off, but I did, and that's that. Anyway, I planted them last night. I didn't think they'd work, but - well, see for yourself. I tried to tell you, but couldn't get a word in edgeways. Come on. Let's go and take a look at the beanstalk."

Out they went into a shining morning. There it stood, a great, dark, towering mass, rearing high into a sky of washed-out blue.

Crabbit took off from Jack's shoulder and landed on a lower branch. In a moment, his black eyes gleamed out at them from between the leaves. He had a caterpillar in his beak.

"Just like the last time," said Jack's ma faintly, craning her neck back in a vain attempt to see the top.

Jack didn't speak. He was remembering the last occasion when he had slipped and slithered down just such a beanstalk at great speed, branches bending and snapping beneath his flying feet. How his heart had hammered as his ears filled with the terrible roaring coming from above. How the beanstalk had swayed and quivered, straining to remain upright beneath the crushing weight of—

"Of course, you're not going up it," said his ma, breaking into his thoughts.

"Why not?" said Jack.

"Because I said so. You might be a lazy layabout with a brain like rice pudding, but you're still my son. I'm not having you eaten by a hulking great giant! Whatever would the neighbours say?"

"I killed the giant, remember?" Jack reminded her. "That's why I'm called Jack the Giant Killer."

"Ah, but there might be others up there."

"Not that I saw. Only the giant's wife.

She's a good sort. A vegetarian."

"So *she* says," said his ma with a sniff. "If she's a vegetarian, what was she doing making bacon sandwiches?"

"They were for the giant. I told you, they had nothing in common."

Jack was walking around the beanstalk, squinting up into the green glare of the leaves, measuring it for size. He grabbed a branch, bent it and let it spring back.

"Oi! Watch it!" protested Crabbit, who was foraging for woodlice or something equally unpleasant.

Jack didn't even notice. He placed one foot on the lowest limb.

"Seems strong enough," he announced with the air of an expert.

"That's as maybe. You're not going up, and that's final."

"Ah, come on, Ma. It's a golden opportunity. We can't let it pass. I know where the treasure chest is and where the giant's wife keeps the key. It's just a question of up, in, grab what I can, out and down again."

"No. Over my dead body."

"But, Ma! There's loads more stuff up

there, Ma. I know. I saw it. Bags and bags of gold. And jewels and silver chalices and crowns and stuff. Ropes of pearls. Diamond rings. Why, I wouldn't mind betting that one of those rings would be enough to put a down-payment on the palace again. Just think! No more washing. Another gold-plated toilet."

His ma hesitated.

"Well . . ." she said slowly. "If you put it like that . . ."

"So I can?"

"All right. But . . . hey! Where are you going?"

Jack was racing back into the house.

"Shan't be a minute! Just getting something!" he shouted and vanished inside.

"The impetuosity of youth, eh?" remarked Crabbit, with a leer.

"You be quiet," snapped Jack's ma who, like Jack, felt uncomfortable around talking birds. Particularly clever dick ones who used long words like 'impetuosity'.

Jack was back in under a minute, stuffing something into his pocket.

"Emergency kit," he explained cheerfully.

And before she could say another thing, he blew her a dramatic kiss, spat on his hands, and sprang at the beanstalk.

The second Jack felt the first sturdy branch beneath his feet and the dark leaves brush against his face, he felt that old, magical surge of energy. This was more like it! For the first time in ages, his head was clear. He felt fit, strong and ready for anything. Surely, confidently, he began to climb.

"Only go for the obvious, mind!" came his ma's anxious voice from below. Steer clear of all that magical rubbish. I don't want any more hens or harps, d'you hear?"

"Right!"

"See if they've got any nice candlesticks! We could do with a decent candlestick."

"I will," promised Jack, climbing swiftly. He was already higher than the cottage roof. He could see the downs in the distance, with that reassuring bulge where the Giant was buried. Whatever adventure lay at the top, it certainly wouldn't involve him.

"And gold! Don't forget the gold, mind!"

"I won't."

"I'm proud of you, Jack! Mother's proud of you!"

Her voice was sounding fainter. Jack paused for a moment astride a branch and looked down. His ma's body had disappeared and he saw only her upturned face watching him anxiously.

"Go on in and make a nice pot of tea!" he shouted, giving a cheery little wave. "I'll be back before you've eaten the last barley cake."

She called out something in reply. It sounded rather like, "I've eaten it already." But the wind took her words and tossed them away and he couldn't be sure. Then the thick foliage blocked his view of her and, once again, it was just him, the sky and the beanstalk.

From now on, the only way was up.

CHAPTER SIX

THE CLIMB

In which Our Hero scales the heights

It was easy at first. A light breeze fanned Jack's face and neck as he climbed, steadily and methodically, ever upward. He got the distinct sense that he was already un-naturally high, with nothing but air and several hundred feet of overgrown plant between him and the fast receding ground.

The one thing he must not do was look down. Once, back in the old days on a previous climb, he had made the mistake of doing just that. One glimpse had been enough. His stomach had heaved, and he had spent an agonizing hour clinging like a whimpering limpet to the main stem before daring to move on up. If it hadn't been for the caterpillar crawling up his breeches, he would probably still be there today.

He knew better now. With three climbs

behind him, he had become quite an old hand. The trick was to keep going, keep looking up, and stay confident.

Crabbit came swooping back from his latest foray for flying bugs and landed on a branch just above him.

"You're slow," he observed flatly. "I thought you'd been up one of these before. Not *that* branch, idiot! It's obvious it won't support your weight."

"Look," said Jack. "When I want your opinion, I'll ask for it. I think I know how to—"

With a little snap, the branch supporting his left foot gave way. His leg dangled horribly in mid air before his flailing foot found another, stouter resting place.

"Told you," crowed Crabbit.

"Shut up."

Mouth set in a grim line, Jack climbed on. Reach - grasp - pull - hoist. Reach - grasp - pull - hoist. He'd got a good rhythm going now.

"Comin' into the clouds soon," remarked Crabbit, after a bit. "I hope you've got a warm vest on."

Sure enough, tendrils of damp mist

began to drift around them. Within minutes, everything was blotted out.

On and up he climbed, finding each new hold by feel alone. His hair was sticky with sap and his arms and legs were beginning to ache unbearably. Despite the cold mist, he was streaming with sweat and his slippery palms more than once failed to grip. Leaves fluttered down and stuck to his wet forehead as he forced himself ever onwards and upwards, hand after white knuckled hand, foot after fumbling foot.

And all the time, Crabbit, as fresh as a daisy, hopped easily from branch to branch above his head, making rude remarks whenever he made a mistake or paused for a breather.

Time dragged by. Jack's stomach rumbled with hunger and his throat was parched. He wished he'd thought of bringing a water bottle.

He had almost given up hope of ever reaching the top, when, suddenly, his head burst through the clouds into dazzling sunlight!

"Made it, then," croaked Crabbit, flapping around his head. "Took enough time, mind."

Yes. There it was: the long, white, familiar road which carved a straight path through the heaped cottonwool cloud mountains, leading directly to the vast, stone, turreted castle which squatted in the distance.

Jack hoisted himself up the last few feet and stepped onto hard white gravel which crunched in a pleasantly solid way beneath his feet.

If his mouth hadn't been so dry, he would have kissed it.

Crabbit swooped down and landed on his shoulder.

"Well?" he demanded. "What's the plan? I take it you've got one?"

"Wait and see," said Jack. And, with slightly wobbly legs but a great deal of determination, he set off towards the castle.

Actually, he wasn't at all sure what he would do when he got there. On previous occasions, made reckless by the glorious smell of frying bacon, he had boldly strode up to the great iron gates and knocked. But this time, he wasn't at all sure of his reception. Circumstances had changed. The giant was no more, and there was no telling how his wife would react.

Luck was on his side. When he reached the great stone arch, the gates stood wide open. He crept into the shadow of the arch and peeped into the courtyard. It was deserted. Just as he remembered, there was a flight of stone steps on the other side, leading up to a studded oaken door.

Heart in his mouth, he scuttled across the open space and hoisted himself up onto the first step. He rested, panting, for a moment -

then heaved himself onto the next - then the third - only one more to go - then, with a gigantic effort, he crawled onto the top step, shutting his eyes for a moment in relief.

And then, suddenly, the air went cold as a mighty shadow fell upon him. He opened his eyes and found his nose inches away from a pair of enormous, shabby tartan slippers sporting grubby pompoms the size of his head!

"WELL NOW," said the giant's wife. "THERE YOU ARE. I WAS WONDERING WHEN YOU'D TURN UP."

CHAPTER SEVEN

THE GIANTESS

In which Our Hero is reunited with an old friend

She had put on weight. There was no doubt about that. Her apron strings strained around her stout middle and several more chins had accumulated beneath her huge red face. Her hair was in a mess too. It hung down in a matted frizz, quite unlike the tidy grey curls that Jack remembered from their previous encounters.

There were, he noticed, a number of stains on her shapeless cardigan. Chocolate, by the look of it. One of the buttons, the size of a small plate, dangled from a loose thread.

But despite it all, she looked quite cheerful.

"WHAT'S THAT ON YOUR SHOULDER?" she enquired. "A FLY, OR SOMETHING?"

"A crow," Jack told her. "But feel free to

swat it if you like," he added helpfully.

"Thanks a lot," muttered Crabbit into his ear.

"WELL, COME ON IN IF YOU'RE COMING," said the giantess, turning and slopping into the castle. Jack followed behind, his hair blowing in the draught from her ill-fitting slippers.

The long, gloomy hall was dirtier than he remembered it. Cobwebs festooned the enormous suits of rusty armour that lined the walls, and dust lay everywhere. With a twinge of guilt, he spotted the familiar portrait of the deceased giant hung on the far wall. He was posing in a loin cloth on a mountain top, thumping his mighty chest and brandishing his favourite nail-studded club.

"TALBOT," said the giantess, pausing and jerking her head. "GOOD LIKENESS, DON'T YOU THINK?"

"I certainly do," agreed Jack with a little gulp.

Talbot? Had that been his name?

He walked quickly past the painting, purposefully avoiding the accusing, painted eyes that peered out through the matted fringe of hair.

"THE PLACE IS A BIT OF A SHAM-BLES," remarked the giantess over her shoulder. "I NEVER WAS ONE FOR HOUSE-WORK. TALBOT WAS THE FUSSY ONE. YOU WOULDN'T THINK SO, WOULD YOU? I MEAN, IN MOST RESPECTS HE WAS A TOTAL SLOB. WELL, YOU'VE SEEN HIM EAT."

"Yes," said Jack with an inward shudder. "Yes, I have."

"HORRIBLE, WASN'T IT?" mused the giant's wife. "ENOUGH TO TURN YOUR STOMACH. 'USE A SPOON,' I'D SAY - BUT HE WOULDN'T. AND ALL THAT STOMP-ING ABOUT BEATING HIS CHEST AND *FEE FI FO FUMMING* ALL OVER THE PLACE. PRIMITIVE, I'D CALL IT. WOULD-N'T YOU?"

"Oh, I wouldn't go so far as to say *that* . . ." Jack began.

"I WOULD. YOU'D THINK HE WAS BORN IN A CAVE. WELL, COME TO THINK OF IT, HE WAS. BUT HE DID LIKE ME TO KEEP THE PLACE LOOKING NICE. BIT OF POLISH, FEW FLOWERS AROUND,

YOU KNOW THE SORT OF THING."

She opened the door to the kitchen. "'COURSE, ME, I COULDN'T CARE LESS. NOW TALBOT'S GONE, I'VE REVERTED TO TYPE - AND A BLOOMIN' RELIEF IT IS TOO! IN YOU COME THEN, I'LL DO YOU A BITE TO EAT."

"Well, if you're sure it's no trouble . . ."

"TROUBLE? OH, NO, IT'S NO TROUBLE. AS A MATTER OF FACT, IT'S NICE TO HAVE A BIT OF COMPANY. I DON'T MIND ADMITTING THE TIME DRAGS A BIT SOMETIMES."

The kitchen was cheerful, as slums go. A fire burned in the huge hearth, casting its light on the piles of unwashed dishes littering every surface. There were, Jack noticed, several empty boxes of chocolates the size of packing cases lying about on the table. A vast, ancient wireless crackled out dance music in one corner.

"I LIKE A BIT OF MUSIC," explained the giant's wife. "SOMETHING TO BREAK UP THE SILENCE, YOU KNOW? BIT OF LIFE. I'M THINKING OF GETTING A CAT."

"Good idea," said Jack. "I don't know

what I'd do without Norman."

"Better," said Crabbit, with feeling. "You'd do better. Believe me."

"WHAT'S YOUR BIRD SAY?"

"He's remarking how much he loves cats," explained Jack, with a sideways glare.

"OH. TALBOT DIDN'T. ALLERGIC. THE HAIRS BROUGHT ON HIS HAY FEVER."

Hay fever? thought Jack wonderingly. What a sensitive hothouse flower the giant had been, underneath all that matted hair.

"MIND YOU, I'M NOT COMPLAIN-ING," went on the giantess. "I'VE GOT ME CHOCOLATES AND ME CROSSWORDS. AND THERE'S BINGO ON TUESDAYS. I GO WITH MRS THUNDERTHIGHS DOWN THE ROAD."

"Well, well, well," marvelled Jack. "Bingo, eh? You're really living it up, then."

"OH, I WOULDN'T SAY *THAT*. BUT I DO GET OUT A BIT. MORE THAN I DID WITH TALBOT. YOU WOULDN'T CATCH HIM GOING OUT, EXCEPT FOR A PINT DOWN THE *THREE OGRES*. YOU'D NEVER GET HIM INTO A SUIT. HE WAS A LOIN

CLOTH MAN, THROUGH AND THROUGH. JUST AS WELL, REALLY, THE AMOUNT OF FOOD HE SPILLED DOWN HIMSELF! NOW THEN. WHERE WOULD YOU LIKE TO SIT? SHALL I POP YOU ON THE TABLE?"

"Yes, please."

She stooped down and gently, ever so gently, took Jack between her thumb and forefinger. He found himself rising through the air, higher and higher, and then his feet touched the table's wooden surface and she released him.

He looked around for something to sit on.

"TRY THE SALT CELLAR," suggested the giantess, pointing. "THAT LOOKS JUST ABOUT THE RIGHT HEIGHT FOR A LIT-TLE FELLER LIKE YOU."

It was, too. Jack flopped down onto it, glad to take the weight off his feet. Crabbit hopped down from his shoulder and began to stroll about the cluttered surface, pecking at outsized toast crumbs.

"COCONUT BUTTER DO YOU?" rumbled the giant's wife, ambling about the

kitchen like a mountain on the move, open-
ing cupboard doors and taking out various
tubs the size of beer barrels. "OR WOULD
YOU PREFER BIGBERRY JAM? ALTHOUGH,
COME TO THINK OF IT, I BELIEVE I
FINISHED THAT OFF."

"No, no, coconut butter will be just fine,"
Jack assured her. "And a glass of water, if it's
not too much trouble. It's a long, hard climb
up the beanstalk."

"A LONG, HARD FALL DOWN TOO, I SHOULDN'T WONDER," remarked the giant's wife meaningfully, hacking away at a mighty loaf with a bread knife that, in Jack's world, could have felled trees.

There was an awkward silence. It went on and on. Jack felt he had to end it.

"Look," he said. "Look, I'm sorry about the gi . . . your hus . . . Talbot. It's just that he was coming after me with his club, and—"

"AH, SAY NO MORE," cried the giant's wife cheerily, slapping something out of a barrel onto a piece of bread the size of a door mat. "HE HAD IT COMING TO HIM. I ALWAYS SAID THAT. 'YOU'LL COME A CROPPER ONE OF THESE DAYS,' I TOLD HIM. HE ALWAYS WAS BAD TEMPERED, YOU KNOW. IT WAS ALL THAT RED MEAT. INDIGESTION, SEE. SHOCKING WIND HE GOT, ESPECIALLY AFTER EATING TITCHIES. I HAD TO LEAVE THE ROOM SOMETIMES. WHY ELSE DID YOU THINK I KEPT YOU HIDDEN FROM HIM?"

"Actually, I thought you were just being kind," said Jack, rather hurt. "I didn't realise it was because you didn't want me to bring on his wind."

"WELL, THAT TOO," confessed the giantess rather shyly. "I'VE ALWAYS HAD A SOFT SPOT FOR YOU TITCHIES."

There fell another little silence.

"Anyway," said Jack. "I really am sorry."

"APOLOGY ACCEPTED. ANYWAY, TO TELL YOU THE TRUTH, I'M NOT SORRY TO SEE THE BACK OF ALL THAT HOUSE-WORK. AND I CAN EAT WHAT I LIKE.

CHOCOLATE, MAINLY. TALBOT WAS ALWAYS TELLING ME THEY'D MAKE ME FAT. 'I'M SUPPOSED TO BE FAT,' I TOLD HIM. 'I'M A GIANTESS. GIANTESSES ARE MEANT TO BE BIG BONED.'"

"They most certainly are. And yours are the biggest bones I've ever seen."

"REALLY? YOU THINK SO?" said the giant's wife, pleased. "YOU DON'T THINK I SHOULD CUT DOWN, THEN? MRS THUNDERTHIGHS IS TALKING ABOUT JOINING FAT FIGHTERS, BUT I KEEP PUTTING IF OFF."

"It'd be a crime," said Jack firmly. "A fine woman like you."

"ANYWAY," continued the giantess, slapping the sandwich onto a plate the size of a dustbin lid, "TALBOT COULDN'T TALK. SHOCKING STOMACH HE HAD ON HIM."

"Mmmm," said Jack guiltily, thinking of the new sledging run up on the downs.

"NOW, I'VE GOT A THIMBLE SOMEWHERE THAT'LL DO FOR YOUR WATER. WHERE'S MY MENDING BOX, I WONDER? IT'S SOME TIME SINCE I'VE DONE ANY MENDING."

"In the cupboard, perhaps?" suggested Jack helpfully. "The one next to the dresser? Where you keep the chest with all the . . . you know. Ahem. Treasure?"

"TREASURE? WHAT TREASURE?"

"You know. The bags of gold. And the jewels and stuff. And the - er - magical bits and bobs."

"OH, *THAT*." The giantess sounded amused. "THAT'S ALL GONE. I SPENT IT."

"Really?" said Jack, crestfallen. He looked around the squalid kitchen, seeking vainly for a sign of house improvements. "Um - what on?"

"CHOCOLATE," admitted the giant's wife. "IT'S HARD TO GET AROUND THESE PARTS. HAS TO BE IMPORTED UP, YOU SEE. I SUPPOSE I OUGHT TO HAVE SAVED A BIT, THERE'S A LOT NEEDS

DOIN' TO THE PLACE. I COULD HAVE
DONE IT UP AN' SOLD IT AN' GOT
MESELF ONE OF THEM NICE BUNGA-
LOWS." She broke off, gave a wistful little
sigh, then determinedly brightened up.
"BUT THERE YOU GO, I DIDN'T, AND
THAT'S THAT. NO POINT IN CRYIN'
OVER SPILT MILK. GOTTA MAKE THE
BEST OF THINGS, HAVEN'T YOU? HERE'S
YOUR SANDWICH. YOU'LL HAVE TO
DRINK YOUR WATER OUT OF AN EGG
CUP, IT'S THE BEST I CAN D–"

But just then, there came an interruption.
There was the clip-clop of hooves from the
courtyard outside. Although clip-clop wasn't
quite the right word. It was more a series of
earth-shattering thuds, suggesting that the
animal to which the hooves were attached
was considerably larger than any horse has a
right to be.

"What's that?" cried Jack, leaping up off
the salt cellar in alarm.

"Uh-oh," muttered Crabbit, hastily flapping onto his shoulder. "Trouble, I think."

The giant's wife glanced through the
window.

"OH NO," she said. "BOTHERATION! I'D FORGOTTEN THEY WERE COMING TODAY. AND THEY'LL BE EXPECTING LUNCH, AND ME WITHOUT A THING IN THE HOUSE."

"Who? What? Who?" cried Jack wildly.

"MY BROTHER EBNER AND HIS FAMI-LY. HAVEN'T I EVER MENTIONED EBNER?"

"No," said Jack heavily. "I don't think you have."

"TELL YOU WHAT," said the giantess. "I THINK YOU'D BE BEST OFF HIDING IN THE OVEN. JUST FOR SAFETY'S SAKE. EBNER'S ALL RIGHT, BUT HE'S NOT SOFT-HEARTED LIKE ME. YOU KNOW THE WAY, DON'T YOU?"

Yes. Jack knew the way all right.

CHAPTER EIGHT

THE RELATIONS

In which Our Hero keeps a low profile

Jack crouched in the rank darkness, up to his ankles in grease. Oven cleaning clearly didn't rank high on the giantess's list of priorities. Thick dollops of congealed fat hung down from the shelves high above his head. The bottom was a foul sea of charred bits of old bacon rind and pools of cold, gluey stew. Luckily, she had left the door open a crack, so at least he could breathe.

Footsteps were approaching now. Huge, clumping footsteps. And he could hear voices. A thunderous, crashing medley of voices topped with a kind of high pitched keening that drilled into your head, making your teeth rattle.

To his horror, the kitchen door opened and in filed four enormous giants - or, to be strictly accurate, two enormous giants (one male, one female), one not quite so enormous but nevertheless unpleasantly large giant, sporting long pigtails and a vast pink frilly dress (female again) and one bald, screaming, wriggling one clasped in the enormous female's arms (sex indeterminate, apart from the clue that it wore blue bootees).

"Sufferin' sparrows!" muttered Crabbit, sounding shocked. "Look at that baby! I hope I'm not around when they change the nappy on that one."

"Ssssh," hissed Jack, reaching up and firmly pinching his beak shut.

"YUCK," boomed the be-pigtailed one rudely, wrinkling her nose. "IT'S POOEY IN HERE."

She began circling the kitchen, opening cupboard doors and picking up things that didn't belong to her.

"DON'T SAY THAT WORD, EUGENIA," scolded the enormous female. She stood wrestling with the shrieking monster baby, looking around the sordid kitchen with an air of disapproval.

She was enveloped from neck to ankle in

what can only be described as a kind of floral marquee and appeared to be wearing a fruit bowl on her head. It was a riot of cherries, oranges and bananas, all topped off with a bit of net to keep the flies away. Over one arm she carried an enormous green handbag, and her vast feet spilled out of matching green shoes with tiny little heels.

"I TAKE IT YOU WEREN'T EXPECTING US, THEN, VI?" she remarked with a curl of the lip.

"YES I WAS," lied the giantess. "BEEN LOOKING FORWARD TO IT ALL MORNING, EDNA."

"SO HOW ARE YOU KEEPING, THEN, SIS?" bellowed the enormous male, clapping the giantess heavily on the back. He was exploding out of a tight, bottle-green, Sunday-Go-Visiting suit, which he had unwisely teamed with a bright yellow shirt and violent purple tie. Jack noticed that his boots squeaked when he walked. His hair was slicked down flat on his head, and there were several bits of paper sticking to his chin, where he had cut himself shaving. He had an uncomfortable air, as though he would be more at home in an old tarpaulin laced with string.

"NOT SO DUSTY, THANKS, EBNER," said the giantess. She began drifting about vaguely, like an untethered barrage balloon, clearing places for everyone to sit.

"GOOD, GOOD, THAT'S MY GIRL," said the giant heartily. He made to sit down at the table.

"DON'T SIT ON THAT BENCH, EBNER," commanded his wife sharply. "THERE'S JAM OR SOMETHING. IF YOU MUST, PUT DOWN A HANKY. YOU'RE WEARING YOUR GOOD SUIT, REMEMBER?"

"IT'S A POOEY SUIT," observed the be-pigtailed one, crashing about in the cupboards.

"STOP USING THAT WORD, EUGENIA, I'VE TOLD YOU BEFORE. AND WHERE ARE YOUR MANNERS? GIVE YOUR AUNTY VIOLET THE NICE PRESENT WE BROUGHT HER."

Violet? *Violet*? That tiny little purple flower that peeped shyly from the hedgerows? Was that really the giantess's name? Jack was learning more and more.

Eugenia sulkily held out a small (well, small in giant terms) parcel, wrapped in brown paper.

"WHAT'S THIS?" said the giantess. (Violet! Jack couldn't get over it.) "CHOCOLATES OR SOMETHING?"

"OH DEAR ME NO. I DON'T THINK WE NEED ANY MORE OF *THOSE*, DO WE,

DEAR?" remarked Edna, with a spiteful glance at her sister-in-law's mighty waistline. "NO, THIS IS SOMETHING YOU'LL TREASURE FOR EVERMORE. WON'T SHE, EBNER?"

"EH?" muttered Ebner, spreading out a none-too-clean hanky on the bench and sitting on it with some relief because his boots hurt.

"I SAID SHE'LL TREASURE OUR GIFT FOR EVERMORE. WON'T SHE, MAXWELL? WON'T AUNTY VIOLET LIKE THE LOVE-LY PREZZY-WEZZY WE GOT HER?"

"NO SHE WON'T," sneered Eugenia. "IT'S A POOEY PRESENT."

"DON'T SAY THAT WORD, EUGENIA," snapped her mother.

Everyone stood and watched as Violet unwrapped the gift and stared at it, expressionless.

"IT'S A FRAMED PHOTOGRAPH OF MAXWELL," explained Edna, "IN HIS BATH, WITH HIS RUBBER DUCKY-WUCKY. THAT'S YOU, ISN'T IT, MAXWELL?"

"WAAAAAAAAAAAAAAAAAAAAH!" squalled her offspring, hurling itself sideways in a kamikaze bid to get down.

"HE'S TEETHING," explained Edna.

"LOVELY," said the giant's wife with a little sigh, putting the photograph down in the butter.

"WHAT'S FOR DINNER, AUNTY VI?" enquired Eugenia suddenly. "I DON'T SMELL ANYTHING COOKING."

And to Jack's horror, she began to walk towards the stove.

"THERE'S ISN'T ANYTHING COOKING," said Violet, standing firmly in the way. "WE'RE HAVING A COLD BUFFIT."

"BUFFIT? WHAT'S THAT, THEN VI?" thundered Ebner, scratching beneath his too-tight suit and loosening his horrible tie.

"DON'T SHOW YOUR IGNORANCE, EBNER. IT'S FRENCH," said his wife.

"OOH LA LA! VERY POSHE," said Ebner. "WHAT IS IT? PICKLED ONION SELLER?"

He guffawed heartily, setting the plates on the dresser rattling.

"NO," said Violet. "COCONUT BUTTER SANDWICHES. I WAS JUST MAKING MYSELF ONE WHEN YOU ARRIVED."

"YUCK!" said Eugenia, making a face. "I HATE COCONUT BUTTER. IT'S POOEY."

"DON'T SAY THAT WORD, EUGENIA," said Edna automatically. Adding, with an air of pride, "SHE'S A TERRIBLY DAINTY EATER. SHE GETS IT FROM MY SIDE OF THE FAMILY."

At this point, the giant baby let fly with a particularly ear-splitting screech of frustration.

In the oven, Jack clapped his hands over his ears and Crabbit stuck his head beneath a wing.

"I SHOULD STICK 'IM DOWN. LET 'IM CRAWL ABOUT," advised Ebner.

"WHAT, ON *THIS* FLOOR? IN HIS LOVELY NEW BABYGRO?" cried his wife, scandalized. "ARE YOU *MAD*, EBNER?"

"WE WON'T GET NO BLINKIN' PEACE TILL YOU DO," said Ebner. "DON'T MIND IF I TAKE ME BOOTS OFF, DO YOU, VI?"

"DON'T YOU DARE, EBNER!" snapped Edna. "TAKING YOUR BOOTS OFF WHEN WE'VE COME FOR LUNCH. THE VERY IDEA!"

"VI DON'T MIND. DO YOU, SIS?"

"BE MY GUEST," said Violet with a shrug.

"OH WELL," sniffed Edna. "IF IT'S GOING TO BE ONE OF *THOSE* OCCASIONS, I SUPPOSE I MIGHT AS WELL LET HIM CRAWL AROUND IN THE FILTH."

She set the screeching baby down. Gleefully, he crawled off under the table, where he immediately found a grubby sugar cube and stuffed it into his mouth.

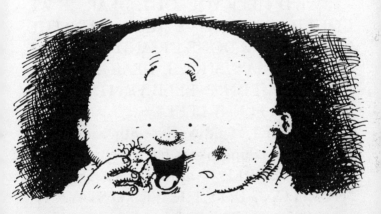

With a little sigh, Edna sat very upright on the edge of her chair with her large green handbag in her lap.

"LOOKS LIKE THE PLACE COULD DO WITH A COAT OF PAINT, VIOLET," she observed, staring around. "IF YOU DON'T MIND MY SAYING SO, DEAR."

"IT COULD, EDNA, IT COULD INDEED," agreed her sister-in-law. "THINGS ARE A BIT TIGHT, THOUGH, SINCE TALBOT'S GONE."

"ARE THEY?" rumbled Ebner. "SORRY TO HEAR THAT, SIS. PERHAPS WE COULD . . . ?"

He glanced at his wife, who shook her head violently and gave him a warning glare.

"WE'D HELP YOU OUT, DEAR, IF WE COULD. BUT WE'VE JUST HAD THE GUEST ROOM DONE UP, AND THE COST OF EUGENIA'S SHOES, DEAR ME, YOU JUST WOULDN'T BELIEVE IT! WE'VE HARDLY A PENNY LEFT."

"I'LL BET," said Violet with a deadpan expression, taking plates from a cupboard.

"I'M BORED," announced Eugenia. "HOW LONG DO WE HAVE TO STAY?"

"SSSH, DARLING," said her mother. "WE'RE STAYING FOR LUNCH."

"I DON'T WANT LUNCH. I'M NOT HUNGRY."

"WELL YOU SHOULD BE," growled Ebner, easing his boots off under the table. "YOU'RE A GIANT, AINCHA? OUGHT TO

86

HAVE A GIANT APPETITE."

"YOU LEAVE HER BE, EBNER," said his wife. "JUST BECAUSE SHE DOESN'T EAT HALF A BUFFALO EVERY MORNING LIKE YOU DO."

Eugenia was still wandering around the kitchen, fiddling with things. Once again, she was coming near the oven. Jack backed away from the door, tripping over a cold chop bone in his haste.

"DON'T GO NEAR THE OVEN, DAR-LING," boomed her mother.

"WHY NOT?" said Eugenia.

"IT'S GREASY. YOU'LL SPOIL YOUR DRESS."

"SO?" said Eugenia. "IT'S A POOEY DRESS."

And she took hold of the door handle.

"Whoops," croaked Crabbit. "Time to make myself scarce. See you later, son."

And suddenly, Jack found his shoulder empty. In the same instant, light poured in in a blinding flash and he put his hands up to shield his eyes. Blinking back tears, he cautiously opened his fingers just a little - and wished he hadn't.

Filling the horizon was a great, looming pink face. Two vast orbs swivelled in their sockets and locked onto him. Two big lips parted slowly to reveal a picket fence of non too clean teeth.

"AUNTY VIOLET," said Eugenia slowly, licking her lips like the cat that ate the cream. "DID YOU KNOW THERE'S A TITCHY IN YOUR OVEN?"

CHAPTER NINE

THE DISCOVERY

In which Our Hero endures rough treatment

"DON'T BE SILLY, EUGENIA," said Edna with a little laugh. "WHAT WOULD A TITCHY BE DOING IN YOUR AUNTY'S OVEN? WHAT AN IMAGINATION YOU DO HAVE."

"THERE IS, I TELL YOU!"

Eugenia reached in with her thumping great hand. Jack sucked in his stomach and tried to press himself through the back of the oven as the seeking fingers advanced, bearing down upon him like the tentacles of a monster octopus - but in vain. Her fist closed triumphantly around him, squeezing the breath out of his lungs. His feet left the floor and he found himself being scooped up and whistled through the air at dizzying speed.

"LOOK!" shrieked Eugenia, displaying him triumphantly. "SEE?"

"You let me go!" yelled Jack at the top of his voice. "You put me down this minute!"

"OH, AND LISTEN! HE TALKS!" honked Eugenia, quite beside herself with delight. "DID YOU HEAR HIS SQUEAKY LITTLE VOICE? YOU JUST SQUEEZE HIS MIDDLE, LIKE THIS, AND HE TALKS!"

She squeezed.

"Eeeeek!" wheezed Jack as the breath shot out of him.

"I'M GOING TO CALL HIM SQUEAKY," announced Eugenia. "HE'S GOING ALL RED, LOOK. HE'S OVEN REDDY. HA, HA! HEAR WHAT I SAID? I SAID OVEN REDDY."

"MAMMOTHS AND MOUNTAINS! I DO BELIEVE SHE'S RIGHT!" spluttered Edna, rising to her feet. "DID YOU KNOW THERE WAS A TITCHY IN THE OVEN, VIOLET?"

"OH, IS THERE?" said the giantess, affecting vague surprise. "ONE OF TALBOT'S LEFTOVERS, I SUPPOSE. I NEVER THOUGHT TO LOOK."

"GREAT!" boomed her brother enthusiastically. "YOU CAN FRY 'IM UP, VI. I'LL 'AVE 'IM. LITTLE BIT OF SALT AND PEPPER, GO DOWN A TREAT."

"WAAAAAH!" bawled Eugenia, great tears spurting from her eyes. "DON'T LET HIM, MA! DON'T LET PA EAT SQUEAKY!"

"NOW SEE WHAT YOU'VE DONE, EBNER. DON'T CRY, DARLING, PA'S ONLY TEASING. HE'S NOT A BARBARIAN LIKE YOUR UNCLE TALBOT. EXCUSE ME, VIOLET, BUT YOU'VE GOT TO ADMIT IT."

"OH, I DO," said Violet cheerfully.

"NO HE WASN'T," argued Ebner stoutly. "HE WAS ALL RIGHT, WAS OLD TALBOT. A BIT ROUGH AND READY, BUT HE ALWAYS BOUGHT HIS ROUND."

"WELL, YOU'RE NOT EATING THE

TITCHY, AND THAT'S THE END OF IT," snapped Edna firmly. "WE PUT ASIDE ALL THOSE OLD WAYS WHEN WE BOUGHT THE NEW VEGETABLE STEAMER. BESIDES, LOOK AT THE STATE OF HIM. HE'S COVERED IN GREASE."

"THAT'S ALL RIGHT. VI'LL RINSE 'IM OFF UNDER THE TAP, WON'T YOU, SIS?" persisted Ebner, loathe to give up this unexpected little treat.

"LOOK AT THE WAY HIS LITTLE LEGS WIGGLE!" marvelled Eugenia, peering closely at poor Jack. "I WANT HIM, MA. I'M GOING TO KEEP HIM FOR A PET. CAN I? CAN I?"

"WELL, I DON'T KNOW ABOUT THAT, DARLING. YOU'VE ALREADY GOT A PET AT HOME. AND YOU DON'T LOOK AFTER *THAT* PROPERLY."

"BOOOHOOOHOOO!" bawled Eugenia. "I WANT HIM! I FOUND HIM! HE'S MINE! MAXWELL GETS EVERYTHING!"

Jack was finding it increasingly hard to breathe. He was trapped in a solid wall of pink flesh, his arms pinned tightly to his sides, his legs foolishly paddling the air.

There was only one thing he could do. Desperately he opened his mouth and bit down hard into her thumb.

"OUCH!" squawked Eugenia, letting go and sticking her thumb in her mouth. "HE BIT ME! THE LITTLE BLIGHTER BIT ME!"

Jack fell like a stone to the floor, landing heavily on his knees at the feet of baby Maxwell, who made a clumsy grab.

"QUICK!" shrieked Edna. "THE BABY'S GOT HIM! PUT HIM DOWN, MAXWELL, YOU DON'T KNOW WHERE'S HE'S BEEN. DIRTY! DIRTY!"

Luckily, Jack's coating of slippery oven grease saved him, and he was able to wriggle from beneath the baby's clutching, sausages like fingers.

Heart in his mouth, he ran for his life towards the kitchen door, which luckily stood open a crack. In seconds he was around it and racing down the long hall. Again, the grease he had picked up in the oven came to his aid, for he went into a long, spectacular skid that carried him along a lot faster than his legs could run.

Behind him, bellowing voices roared and

thundered as the giants milled around the kitchen, tripping over benches and boots and each other in their haste to get after him.

Jack's skid carried him as far as the main door, which also stood open. Giants, it seemed, weren't big on shutting doors.

Wildly he raced through, tumbled head over heels down the steps (ignoring the pain of bumped head and grazed knees) and hotfooted it across the courtyard, where a horse stood patiently waiting between the traces of a carriage. Like everything else, it was built on a monumental scale. It didn't even notice as Jack dodged between its hooves and scuttled under the archway, where the road to the beanstalk began.

Even as he set foot on the gravel, Jack felt it shake, the millions of little stones resonating as the pursuing Giants thundered across the courtyard. It was all horribly familiar - except that this time, there were *three* of them. Well, four, if you included Maxwell. Violet had stayed behind in her untidy kitchen. She had seen it all before.

Lungs bursting, he stumbled along the path. His legs felt like they were about to drop off and he could feel the beginnings of a stitch. How much further to the beanstalk? He honestly didn't think he could run much longer.

He came upon it unexpectedly. Or rather, he came upon the gaping hole in the clouds where it *had* been. Arms windmilling wildly, he teetered on the edge, staring down in disbelief. Surely it wasn't possible! How could a huge beanstalk simply *disappear*? What great force could have demolished a plant as tall as a mountain in the space of a few, short hours?

As he stood, swaying, at the edge of the hole, the answer came to him. Of course! Why hadn't he thought of it before? He had reckoned without the snails.

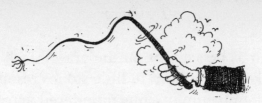

CHAPTER TEN

THE JOURNEY

In which Our Hero goes on a trip

"I'VE GOT A NEW PET, I'VE GOT A NEW PET!" sang Eugenia at the top of her king-sized lungs, gripping Jack firmly around his middle and violently bouncing him up and down on her lap.

They were seated in the giants' carriage, bowling along past great, white, whipped-up banks of candyfloss cloud interspersed with occasional lakes of blue sky.

On the seat opposite, Edna was attempting to restrain Maxwell, who was hanging over her shoulder, gnawing at the brass buttons on the upholstered seat back with his inflamed gums.

Outside and up front, Ebner could be heard cracking the driver's whip and bellowing encouragement to the gigantic horse.

"LOOK, MA, I'M MAKING HIM WALK

ON MY KNEES! WALK, SQUEAKY, WALK!
WHY'S HE STOPPED WALKING? WALK,
SQUEAKY!"

"No," shouted Jack defiantly. "I won't!"

"WALK, OR I'LL POKE YOU WITH MY
HAIRGRIP AGAIN," threatened Eugenia.

"DO PUT HIM AWAY, EUGENIA," said
Edna crossly, yanking Maxwell back down
into her lap, where he squirmed around, red-
faced and open-mouthed, moisture cascad-
ing from every orifice. "JUST LOOK AT THE
MESS HE'S MAKING ON YOUR NICE
DRESS. I'LL NEVER GET ALL THOSE LIT-
TLE GREASY FOOTPRINTS OUT."

"NO," said Eugenia obstinately. "HE'S
MINE. I WANT TO PLAY WITH HIM."

"WELL, AT LEAST WRAP HIM IN A
HANKY OR SOMETHING. HE'S *FILTHY.*"

Jack gave a squawk as Eugenia
caught hold of his ankle with
her thumb and forefinger
and swept him into the air.
She held him dangling
upside down, inches in
front of her huge face,
inspecting him.

"HMM. ARE YOU DIRTY, SQUEAKY? WELL, I SUPPOSE YOU ARE A BIT. NEVER MIND, I SHALL GIVE YOU A BATH IN THE PUDDING BASIN WHEN WE GET HOME."

"Don't you dare!" howled Jack, thrashing with his free leg. There was a roaring in his ears as the blood went rushing to his head. "No great girl's going to bath me!"

"NO TITCHY BATHING UNTIL AFTER TEA," announced Edna firmly. "I MIGHT HAVE KNOWN WE WOULDN'T GET ANYTHING TO EAT AT YOUR AUNT VIOLET'S. I DON'T KNOW WHY WE BOTHER TO GO. THERE'S NEVER ANYTHING PREPARED."

"DINGLE, DINGLE, DANGLE!" sang Eugenia, bobbling Jack up and down. "OOH, LISTEN, MA. LISTEN TO HIS CUTE LITTLE SCREAMS. I'M GOING TO PUT HIM IN THE CAGE WITH PRINCESS TINKLEBELL WHEN WE GET HOME. PERHAPS THEY'LL FIGHT."

Princess Tinklebell? Who, in a world of appalling names, was that?

"YOU'D BETTER PUT HIM IN YOUR POCKET WHEN YOU GET OUT," advised

Edna. "YOU KNOW WHAT YOUR FATHER'S LIKE WHEN HE GETS A FANCY FOR RED MEAT."

The never-ending blue and white scenery flowed past the window. The only difference was that Jack was now viewing it upside down. He had been in some nasty positions in his life. This was, without doubt, one of the worst.

At this point, the rhythmic thump of the horse's hooves began to slow down and the carriage ground to a halt.

"AT LAST!" sighed Edna. "COME ON, MAXWELL, TIME FOR BEDDY-BYES. WE'RE BACK."

"LOOK," said Eugenia, grasping Jack firmly around his middle, turning him the right way up and grinding his nose into the window. "LOOK, SQUEAKY. THIS IS YOUR LOVELY NEW HOME."

The coach had drawn up before another castle. At least, he supposed you would call it a castle in that it had pointy turrets. In all other respects it resembled a wedding cake from hell. It was painted a hideous, sugary pink. Frothy-white lace curtains hung at every window. There was a fountain in the court yard arising from a square pond in which swam goldfish the size of sharks. There was a sign on the wrought iron gate which said:

CLOUDVIEW CASTLE.
STRICTLY PRIVATE.
NO HAWKERS, CIRCULARS
OR DUMPING.

That was all he had chance to see before he found himself whistling through the air again and being roughly stuffed into Eugenia's pocket.

It wasn't pleasant in there. There was hardly room to move amongst the mess of balled-up used tissues and vast, crinkly, sticky old toffee papers all gummed-up with fluff. Exhaustedly, he lay back with his head on a half-eaten beachball-sized gobstopper and tried to think.

CHAPTER ELEVEN

THE PRINCESS

In which Our Hero is caged with royalty

"OUT YOU COME, SQUEAKY," sang Eugenia gaily, and Jack found himself being gripped around the waist by a vast thumb and forefinger and roughly dragged out into the light. Before he could even cry out, he was flying through the air again, landing flat on his back, all the breath knocked out of him. There was the sound of a door clanking shut.

"SEE YOU LATER, SQUEAKY. AFTER I'VE HAD MY TEA. BE PREPARED FOR A NICE, HOT BATH," announced Eugenia. Her thunderous footsteps receded, and all was quiet.

Jack lay there for a moment, feeling sick. Then - slowly, painfully - he eased himself into a sitting position. Every bit of him hurt.

He found himself sitting on the bottom of a cage which had most probably once housed some bloated budgie or walloping great canary or something. The floor was covered in grit. Metal bars rose on all sides. In one corner there was a trough heaped with something that looked like birdseed, although each seed was the size of a small potato. In the opposite corner was a similar trough containing brackish water.

Jack looked up. A short way above his head, running from one side of the cage to the other, was a perch. Clamped to the bars at one end there was a cracked mirror with a bell attached. At the other end was the door. And sitting slap between the two, wearing a long blue dress and a crown, sat a girl. She was swinging her legs and staring down at him with an inscrutable expression.

Jack wasn't at all sure about girls. Back home in the village, they giggled at him, causing his neck to go red and his feet to turn into pastry. Even when he was a hero living in the palace, the noblemen's haughty daughters had looked down their noses at him and sneered about his lack of dancing ability.

This one didn't look giggly, at any rate. Or particularly friendly, if it came to it. He

decided to try his hand at speech.

"Princess Tinklebell, I presume?" said Jack.

"Go boil your head," said the girl coldly. It wasn't a promising opening to a conversation.

"Pardon me for living! Just that I heard the name mentioned, and—"

"Do I *look* like a Princess Tinklebell?" interrupted the girl.

Jack looked up at her. She had no shoes on and her bare feet were unbelievably dirty. On closer examination, the long blue dress was filthy too. In fact, it wasn't so much a dress as a length of material, wrapped around her and secured at the back with an enormous safety pin. The crown too was fake. It looked rather like a cheap toy from a Christmas cracker, with gaping holes where several of the jewels had fallen out. It sat crookedly on top of a shaggy mop of brown hair which from the look of it had been cut by a blind maniac armed with garden shears.

"No," said Jack frankly.

"Well, there you go then. That's just what *she* calls me."

"Well, I'm sorry. I just assumed . . ."

"Well, don't," said the girl. And that appeared to be that.

Painfully, Jack climbed to his feet and brushed himself down as well as he could. Bits of fluff from Eugenia's pocket had adhered to his general coating of grease, and now there was grit as well. Whatever he touched stuck to him. The girl watched in silence as he limped over to the bars and peered out.

The cage was set on a table in what was unmistakably Eugenia's room. She had a mammoth mobile, a wallclock with a gorilla who popped out and thumped his chest on the hour, and an excessively large collection of oversized, stuffed cuddly animals. There was a towering bookcase filled with books bearing titles like *THE WHOPPER BOOK OF FUN* and *TALL TALES FOR BIG GIRLS*. There was a poster of a group of spotty-faced guitar-playing giants with greasy hair called *BULLY BOYZ* on the wall, and another of a female group with big blonde hairdos who were, apparently, *THE LARGEAIRES*.

Between the posters, the wall itself was covered with angry looking scribbles in black crayon. One was of a stick figure with a rope around its neck, labelled: **MaXweL.**

From the look of her vast, unmade bed and the amount of enormous toys, gargantuan shoes, headless dolls and outsized items of discarded clothing scattered about the place, it was clear that Eugenia was untidy in a *big* way.

With a groan of dismay, Jack grasped two of the bars in his hands, took a deep breath and attempted to force them apart.

"There's no point," said the girl. "They're too strong."

"I'll be the judge of that," said Jack primly. He flexed his muscles, planted his feet firmly, gripped the bars and tried again. The veins stood out on his forehead. Sweat trickled down his back. This time, he really put his back into it.

The bars didn't give an inch.

Jack let go with a gasp and waited for the roaring in his ears to subside.

"See?" said the girl smugly. "Told you."

Jack ignored her. He spat on his hands, reached for the perch and, with an effort, managed to haul himself up. He stood swaying slightly, gained his balance after a bit of arm flailing, then teetered along it towards the door.

"It's spring-loaded," said the girl in a know-all fashion. "Don't waste your time."

Jack put his shoulder to it and heaved for all he was worth. The door, of course, stayed firmly shut.

"Careful, Squeaky, you'll do yourself an injury," sneered the girl.

Jack gave up. He sagged against the door and looked at her.

"My name is not Squeaky," he told her. "It's Jack. And I'll thank you to keep your sarcasm to yourself. I've had a bad day."

"You and me both," said the girl. Suddenly she flipped backwards off the perch and hung upside down from her knees. Her crown fell off and dropped to the bottom of the cage, where it rolled around for a bit before settling in a corner.

"Bet you can't do this," said the girl.

"Don't want to," said Jack.

"Even if you did, you couldn't," said the girl. "You haven't had circus training, you see."

"And you have?"

"Of course I have! I was with the Chipolata Brothers for three years. Do you want to see me hang from my big toe?"

"Not particularly," said Jack. But, despite himself, he was impressed. The *Chipolata Brothers' Touring Circus* was the best in the land. He'd heard there were elephants. Jack had never seen an elephant. He had always wanted to go, but had never managed to raise enough money for the entrance fee. Well, that wasn't strictly true. He could have afforded it when he was living at the palace, but his ma hadn't let him. Apparently it wasn't the Done Thing to visit circuses when you lived in a palace, though for the life of him he couldn't see why.

Suddenly the girl jack-knifed herself upwards with an easy movement and was sitting on the perch again.

"Are you usually as dirty as that?" she enquired, wrinkling her nose.

"Only when I've spent the best part of the afternoon hiding in an oven," said Jack defensively. He spat on his finger and rubbed hopelessly at his breeches.

"She'll be up to play with you soon, you know," the girl told him. "She'll bath you first. In the pudding basin. And then she'll dress you in stupid clothes. Probably a dolly's nighty. And then she'll do awful things to your hair. Curl it and put pretty pink ribbons in. That's what she did to me. And when I complained, she lost her temper and cut it off."

"She's not putting ribbons in *my* hair," said Jack stoutly.

"You can't stop her. And then she'll play schools with you. She'll make you do sums and give you marks out of ten, then stick you in a corner with a dunce's hat. Then she might take you for a ride in the doll's pram. Or force feed you birdseed and poke you with a stick until you dance. That's on a good day."

"What happens on a bad day?" asked Jack, not really wanting to know.

"She'll throw you at the wall," said the girl, adding, "Lucky I know how to land. Circus training, you see."

Jack thought about being thrown at the wall by Eugenia. Then he placed his shoulder to the door and pushed again with renewed vigour. The girl watched pityingly until he ran out of steam and was forced to retire, defeated.

"Isn't there any way out of this cage?" he asked.

"No," said the girl. "And even if there was, the bedroom door's too heavy to push open. We're right at the top of a turret, and even if you made it down the steps, you wouldn't last two minutes. The cat sleeps on the doormat in the hall."

"Oh," said Jack. A giant cat. Great. Just great. "You seem to know a lot about everything," he added.

"I ought to," said the girl with a little sigh. "I've been here for weeks."

"Really?" said Jack, adding curiously: "How did you get here in the first place?"

"Shot from a cannon," said the girl. "*Miss Fire, the Amazing Human Cannon Ball*, that's me. Of course, that's just my stage name. My real name's Doreen."

"So what happened?" asked Jack. He had never met a Human Cannon Ball called Doreen before.

"Too much gunpowder, combined with a high wind. I was supposed to come down and land in a net, but I just

110

kept on going. Next thing I knew I was lying in the courtyard looking up Eugenia's nostrils, with her going, 'Ooh, ma, look what *I've* found.' What about you?"

"Climbed up a beanstalk," said Jack, casually.

"Really?" said Doreen. He wasn't sure, but he thought he detected a touch of grudging admiration in her voice.

"Actually, I've done it several times," he continued. "You - er - you might have heard of me. They call me Jack the Giant Killer. This time last year I was quite famous."

"No," said Doreen. "Can't say I have. Of course, we circus people travel round quite a lot. It's hard to keep up with the news. I must say you don't look like a giant killer. If you're a giant killer, how come you've let yourself be captured by one?"

There was no answer to that. He looked down at his fingernails, crestfallen.

"Sorry," said Doreen, quite kindly. "Didn't mean to be rotten. Being a giant's plaything doesn't put you in a very good humour. I expect you were quite a good giant killer. Anyway, I'm sure your experience will come in very useful. I suppose you've got a master-plan or something?"

"No," admitted Jack. "Not really. Come to think of it, it was only luck that saved me last time. Along with my lightning reflexes, of course. And amazing biceps. And quick wits. Combined with the fact that the giant was a particularly stupid one."

And to his surprise, he found himself giving a dry little chuckle.

To his even bigger surprise, Doreen joined in. Perhaps she wasn't such a bad sort after all. Apart from being a bit of a show-off on the acrobatic front.

"Have you got a masterplan, then?" he asked humbly.

"As a matter of fact, I have," said Doreen. "I've had a lot of time to think about it. But first, we have to find a way of getting out of the ca—"

She broke off. There was a slithering noise coming from the doorway of Eugenia's room. And the odd thump. Slithering and thumping, accompanied by heavy, laborious breathing.

"Oh no," said Doreen. "I hope that's not who I think it is."

She froze on the perch. Both their eyes were glued to the massive bedroom door which slowly swung open on shrieking hinges. A big, pink, drooling face appeared low down in the gap. When it spotted the cage, it broke into a delighted, gummy grin.

It was Maxwell!

CHAPTER TWELVE

THE ACCIDENT

In which Our Hero gets rattled

"GROO!" announced Maxwell, by way of an introduction. "BLOOGLE HIC PERTWEE?"

He crawled relentlessly towards the cage.

There was a moment's pause while he disappeared beneath, then a lot of grunting noises as he hauled himself himself unsteadily to his feet. The table supporting the cage wobbled alarmingly - then, to Jack and Doreen's considerable dismay, what seemed like acres of pink baby face rose before them like the sun. Maxwell's button blue eyes ogled them and his excited breath came in milky gusts.

"You leave us alone, Maxwell!" scolded Doreen. "You're not allowed in Eugenia's room! Bad baby! Go away!"

"PEEDLE SHLUP! BAM!" responded Maxwell intelligently, wreathed in smiles.

"POOGLE! BLURP! BAM! BAM! BAM!"

Each bam! was accompanied by an open-handed smack on the cage bars. Jack and Doreen felt their prison shift beneath them.

"Stop it, Maxwell!" screamed Doreen, clinging to her perch for dear life. "I'm telling Eugenia!"

"BLAH!" chortled Maxwell, beside himself with the fun of it all. "SHPLOT! TEE HEE HEE!"

His podgy fingers wrapped themselves around the bars and he rattled the cage for all he was worth.

"Ahhhhhhhh!" shrieked Jack as the floor tilted beneath him. He flung out his hand to grasp the nearest bar, missed, pitched forward and found himself rolling down the gritty slope, coming to a crumpled halt under the seed tray, which obligingly spilled its contents onto his head and shoulders in a steady stream.

"Ally oop!" whooped Doreen, leaping from the perch and attaching herself monkey-like to the bars.

"SCHLOOP! SCHLOOP!" trumpeted Maxwell, giving a final heave. With a grinding noise, the cage finally slid off the table into his arms. The weight, combined with the suddenness of the movement, proved too much for him. His wobbly fat knees gave way and, with a look of surprise, he sat down on his well cushioned bottom. Luckily for its occupants, the cage landed on top of him.

"PLUNKET?" enquired Maxwell. "TACKY POOP. OOOG!"

With a cross gesture, he swept the cage off his lap and onto the floor, where it landed on its side with little crashings and tinklings, spilling birdseed and water onto the carpet.

There was a silence. Slowly, Jack lifted one of the arms he had been using to protect his head and risked a glimpse. The floor had now become a wall, and he was lying on his back across the doorway. The cage bars were now horizontal instead of vertical.

There was no doubt about it. This was an emergency. Talking of which . . .

He thrust his hand deep into his pocket. Was it still there? Could it have fallen out at some point?

No. Much to his relief, his questing fingers closed around the crumpled paper bag.

"Are you all right?" enquired Doreen, clambering down from on high and dropping lightly next to him.

"Never better," said Jack grimly. "You know my bruised ribs? Well, they don't hurt so much now, because I've got this lump growing on my head, and that *really*— Where is he? What's happening? Why's he gone quiet?"

"It's the lull before the storm. He's building up air, and any minute now he's going to let fly with one of his specials. Then everyone'll come running . . . what are you doing?"

Jack was poking about in the bag.

"I've just remembered something. It might be worth a try. Look, stop him raising the alarm, would you?"

"How?"

"I don't know! Distract him. Say nice things to him. We've got to buy ourselves some time. You're a girl. Girls like babies, don't they?"

"Not this girl. Not this baby. What's that you're eating?"

"I don't know yet. Probably a furball pill. Please, Doreen!"

Doreen gave a shrug, then sprang at the perch, which now rose vertically from what was now the floor to what was now the ceiling. Swiftly, she flew up, while down below, Jack choked down the orange pill that Old Mother Skinnard had so thoughtfully provided.

Maxwell still sat on the carpet where he had fallen. His face was a scarlet mask. A purple vein throbbed in his temple. His mouth was open in a perfectly circular O. He'd got all the breath he needed. It had taken a while, but if a thing was worth doing, it was worth doing well. His lungs were now filled to bursting, and all set to blast out a scream of furious protest that would undoubtedly notch up yet another record. Then:

"Maxwell!" cooed a sugary voice from the wreckage of the cage. "Look, Maxwell! What's that over there? On the shelf?"

A tiny hand protruded from between the bars and urgently pointed towards a towering set of shelves in the far corner of the room. Maxwell's brimming eyes rolled slowly in their sockets.

"It's Eugenia's sweety jar, Maxwell. It's got the red sticky ones you're not allowed. Maxwell wants a sweety, doesn't he?"

Maxwell's slow baby brain lumbered into sluggish action. Little electrical impulses trickled along various nerve paths, and saliva slopped into his mouth like an incoming tide. Yes. Maxwell wanted a sweety all right.

"Quick, Maxwell," coaxed the voice. "Quick, before nasty old Eugenia comes. Maxwell's a good baby. He deserves a sweety.

A lovely red sweety, all to himself . . ."

Maxwell let out his saved-up breath in a short, sharp, extremely positive belch. His mouth ceased to be an O, and curved up into a toothless, greedy grin. He flopped over onto his tummy, and set off at a lumbering crawl towards the forbidden fruits of Eugenia's king-sized sweet jar.

"I've a real way with babies," announced Doreen, appearing at Jack's side with an air of triumph. "He's doing it. Just needs a firm hand, that's all. I blame the parents . . . Hey! You've done it!"

"I know," said Jack, flexing his muscles with a certain amount of pride.

He had, too. He had simply stepped up to the bars, grasped hold of two of them and yanked hard. Much to his amazement, they had bent like butter, leaving plenty of space to step through.

"Gosh," said Doreen. "Those furball pills are *good.*"

Together, they stepped through the gap and out onto the soaked, seed-strewn carpet.

On the far side of the room, Maxwell stood unsteadily with his back to them. He had managed to heave himself upright, using the edge of a shelf. Like all babies, his powers of concentration were limited. His little mishap with the cage was forgotten. The little wiggly things that lived in the cage were forgotten. His whole universe now consisted of the forbidden sweet jar, which stood just within reach of his fumbling fingers.

"Now!" instructed Doreen. "Quick, while he's occupied. To the mousehole!"

"What mousehole?"

"Over there, look, in the skirting. By the bed leg. Come on, come on, let's go, before he realises he can't get the top off. Run!"

Jack didn't need telling twice.

CHAPTER THIRTEEN

THE MOUSEHOLE

In which Our Hero shelters from the storm

"You don't think it's inhabited, do you?" whispered Jack, with a little shiver. The tunnel stretched away behind him, black as the inside of a chimney. He stood ankle-deep in the dust of ages, keeping well back from the dim light which filtered in from the room beyond.

"Shouldn't think so. Can't see any fresh droppings. Why? Don't you like mice?"

"Not ones that can knock me over. *Where are you going?*"

His voice held an edge of panic.

"Calm down, will you? I'm just having a look along the tunnel. You never know, it just might lead to the outside. Stay here and keep your eyes peeled. I shan't be long."

Instantly, she was swallowed by the shadows and her echoing footsteps receded into the distance.

Jack dropped to his knees, crawled to the opening and risked a quick look. His view of Maxwell was blotted out by Eugenia's gargantuan bed, but from the sound of the heavy, concentrated breathing coming from the far corner of the room, the monster baby was still very much present.

"No good," said Doreen, coming up behind and making him jump. "There's been a fall. The roof's collapsed. We'll just have to hole up here 'til nightfall. Then we can put my masterplan into operation."

"Ah yes, the masterplan," nodded Jack politely. "You mentioned that. So what would that be, then?"

"It's a bit complicated," explained Doreen. "And risky. It involves quite a bit of climbing, and you'll need nerves of steel."

"Oh, good," said Jack heavily. "That's all right then. At least three minutes have gone by without me being squashed, dropped from a great height, poked with a hairgrip, dangled upside down, stuck-up with toffee papers or buried alive in birdseed. I could do with a bit of excitement."

"Look on the bright side," said Doreen. "At least you've still got your hair. And you don't have to go round with a thumping great safety pin holding your clothes on. And we're out of the cage, that's a good star—"

She broke off.

There came the sound of a resounding crash. It was the kind of sound that a jumbo sized sweet jar makes when it falls from a great height and breaks into a thousand pieces. It was a loud noise. It was an impressive noise. But it was as nothing when compared with the noise that followed.

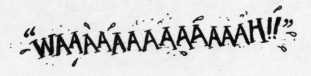

"WAAAAAAAAAAAAAH!!"

"Oooops," said Doreen, with a certain amount of satisfaction. "Maxwell's broken the sweet jar. Now we'll see some action."

There came the sound of distant, pounding feet racing up the stairs. The door burst open, and in raced Eugenia. Her eyes flickered over the carnage and alighted on Maxwell, who lay like a stranded whale in a shallow sea of broken glass and scattered confectionary.

"YOU LITTLE BEAST! YOU HORRIBLE, THIEVING LITTLE WRETCH! YOU'VE BROKEN MY SWEETY JAR!" howled Eugenia. "RIGHT, THAT'S DONE IT, MAXWELL! YOU'VE GONE TOO FAR THIS TIME. I'M GONNA RIP THE ARMS OFF YOUR TEDDY!"

"AND THEN I'M GONNA GET YOUR RUBBER DUCK, AND I'M GONNA . . ."

"STOP THAT, EUGENIA!" Edna came panting into the room, scooped up the felled infant and began joggling him concernedly. "HE'S HURT HIMSELF, THE BLESSED

ANGEL! THERE'S A BIG BUMP ON HIS HEAD!"

"GOOD! THAT'LL LEARN HIM NOT TO COME IN MY ROOM AND MESS AROUND WITH MY THINGS!"

"WHAT'S GOIN' ON?" roared Ebner, clumping in. "WHAT'S THE PESKY LITTLE BLIGHTER GONE AND DONE NOW?"

"DON'T YOU SPEAK TO HIM LIKE THAT! I TOLD YOU TO PUT HIM IN HIS COT! THIS IS ALL YOUR FAULT, EBNER."

"I DID PUT HIM IN HIS COT. LITTLE

DEVIL MUST HAVE CLIMBED OUT."

"LOOK!" screamed Eugenia. "THAT'S NOT ALL HE'S DONE! HE'S PULLED THE CAGE DOWN AND PRINCESS TINKLE-BELL AND SQUEAKY HAVE GOT OUT! WHERE ARE THEY? WHAT HAVE YOU DONE WITH MY PETS, MAXWELL, YOU PIECE OF PIGGY POOP!"

"ARE YOU HEARING THIS, EBNER? ARE YOU HEARING WHAT YOUR DAUGH-TER CALLS HER BABY BROTHER? THERE, THERE, MAXWELL, DON'T CRY,

MUMMY'S HERE."

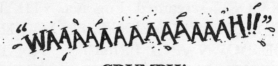

CRUMPH!

"OW!" screamed Edna. "HE BIT ME! BAD, BAD BOY, MAXWELL, YOU MUSTN'T BITE MUMMY! SEE WHAT HE'S DONE? HE'S BITTEN MY FINGER!"

"GIVE 'IM A SMACK, THEN!" boomed Ebner, sounding more than irritable.

"A SMACK? A *SMACK*? WHAT KIND OF A SOLUTION IS THAT? HE'S ALREADY BATTERED, LOOK AT THE LUMP ON HIS PRECIOUS HEAD! THAT'S TYPICAL OF YOU, EBNER, YOU THINK A SMACK SOLVES EVERYTHING."

"SQUEAKY! SQUEAKY! WHERE ARE YOU, SQUEAKY?"

"NEVER MIND YOUR STUPID PETS, EUGENIA, GO AND GET THE BRUSH AND DUSTPAN. THERE'S GLASS ALL OVER THE PLACE."

"SHAN'T! I'M LOOKING FOR PRINCESS TINKLEBELL!"

"DO AS YOUR MOTHER TELLS YOU,

GIRL!"

"NO!"

"DO AS YOUR FATHER TELLS YOU, EUGENIA!"

"NO! SHAN'T! I HATE YOU!"

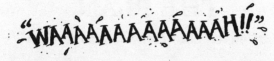

Giants, as might be expected, have BIG rows - and this one was no exception. It went from bad to worse. There were stamped feet and accusations. There were screams, threats, tears and clenched fists. There were, sad to say, quite a few vulgar words delivered at ear-splitting volume, mostly coming from the mouth of Eugenia. The only time Maxwell stopped screaming was in order to fill his nappy, which added yet another thoroughly disagreeable dimension to the whole apalling scene.

In the relative safety of the mousehole, the escapees sat with their backs to the wall and their fingers jammed firmly in their ears as the heavy footsteps clumped to and fro and the roaring voices raged on . . . and on . . . and on . . . and on . . .

CHAPTER FOURTEEN

THE PLAN

In which Our Hero ventures forth

Great, choked snores rent the air. Eugenia, still fully clothed, was sprawled flat out on her bed in a mess of shredded sheets and torn blankets. Her scarlet face, streaked with tears of rage, was buried in the sodden pillow. Every time she breathed out, more feathers escaped from the large hole she had chewed in it.

Moonlight filtered through the smashed window, lighting the shocking scene of devastation. There is nothing like a giant temper tantrum to demolish a room, and Eugenia was a past master.

Everywhere was wreckage and ruin. Everything that could be ripped was torn to shreds. Everything that could be smashed was in smithereens. Headless dolls were now limbless as well. The floor was littered with broken glass, severed plastic arms and legs and sad torsos.

Multicoloured pots of paint had been thrown at the walls and trodden into the carpet. Tables and chairs had been kicked over. The gorilla clock had been torn from the wall and thoroughly stomped on. Posters hung in ribbons. The empty cage lay in the corner where it had been kicked, a tangled mass of bent wires.

In the stuffy darkness of the mousehole, Doreen and Jack slowly removed their hands from their ringing ears.

"Wow!" said Jack at length, his voice dripping with relief plus a hint of admiration. "That's the way to do it."

"I told you, didn't I?" said Doreen. "I said she likes to get her own way."

"Did you see what she did to the cage? And when she got the scissors and disembowled the stuffed giraffe? And when she chucked the doll's pram through the window . . . ?"

"I know. I saw."

"But when she threw all her clothes in a pile and poured ink over 'em! And when she took the hammer to . . ."

"I know, I know. You forget, I've been here longer than you. I've seen it all before. Actually, we're lucky she threw one of her wobblers. It's worked in our favour. She's smashed the window. It'll be easier to carry out my masterplan. How are your ears?"

Jack considered.

"The ringing's died down, but I'm still a bit deaf in one."

"Good. Well, if you're feeling fit, let's get cracking."

"Right. Great. So - er - what do we crack, exactly?"

Doreen scrambled to her feet and moved to the opening. Her tiny face, white in the moonlight, peered cautiously around the skirting board. High above, on the dizzy heights of the bed, Eugenia smacked her lips, mumbled "POOEY!" in her sleep, then continued to snore.

"See up there?" hissed Doreen, pointing into a far corner of the devastated room.

"What? Where?"

Jack climbed groggily to his feet and joined her.

"Up there, look. On top of the wardrobe.

Know what's up there?"

"No. What?"

"Her secret ball of elastic. She uses it to make catapults. They confiscated the last one, but the elastic's still up there."

"So? Why do we need a ball of elas . . . Wait a minute." His eyes flickered to the broken window. "I hope you're not suggesting what I think you are."

"It's the only way," said Doreen. "All we have to do is somehow get the ball of elastic down from the top of the wardrobe, roll it over to the window, make some sort of ramp or something, get it up onto the windowsill and find a sticky-out nail or something to tie it to."

"My word," murmured Jack. "All those 'somehows' and 'somethings'. Every little wrinkle ironed out, eh? You've really given this a lot of thought. Then what do we do? After we've tied this elastic to this incredibly convenient nail? Attach ourselves to the other end and hurl ourselves headfirst out the window?"

"That's right," said Doreen briskly. "It's easy. The clowns do it in the circus all the time. Know what it's called?"

"Certain Death?"

"No, silly! Gungee Jumping. The clowns do it into a barrel of gunge. Goes down very well with the crowds. Anyway, have you got a better plan?"

"No," admitted Jack with a little sigh.

"Let's go, then."

Silently, they slipped from the hole and moved out into the moonlit room. Trying not to breathe, they crept along the length of the giant bed, from which strident snores still issued.

"She's driving her dinosaurs to market," whispered Jack, and Doreen gave a nervous little giggle.

Swiftly, they raced across the vast wastes of the carpet, avoiding the broken glass, clambouring over the wrecked toys, skirting the heaps of ruined clothes and ducking under the overturned items of furniture.

The towering wardrobe stood on the far side of the room. It rose up almost to the ceiling, its sides as sheer and slippery as a glass mountain. The top seemed as inaccessible as the moon.

They stood at the foot, staring up.

"Doreen," said Jack, after a moment's contemplation. "There is no way we can climb up that."

"We've got to," said Doreen. "We need that elastic. It's our only chance. You haven't still got your super strength, by any chance?"

"I don't know. Why?"

"Try lifting the wardrobe. Perhaps you can shake it off."

Jack set his shoulder against the gargantuan wardobe and tried lifting it.

It was painfully obvious that his super strength had deserted him.

"Sorry," he gasped. "It seems to be all used up."

"Haven't you got anything else magical in your pocket?"

"Well," said Jack, with a little blush.

"Ahem. A bottle of Love Potion."

Doreen looked unimpressed.

"Anything else?"

"A pair of Seven League Socks. But I've got a feeling they're not supposed to be used for jumping up to the top of wardrobes. You've got to be careful with these magical things. You have to use them at the right time. Besides, they're smelly. What we really need is a pair of wings. "

"Ah," remarked a sudden voice from the windowsill above, making them both jump. "My cue, I think."

There was a flapping, a whoosh, and suddenly Jack's shoulder was gripped by a familiar set of sharp claws.

"Oh," said Jack, coldly. "It's you again. I was wondering where you got to. A fine help you've turned out to be when the chips were down."

"No need to get shirty," croaked Crabbit, huffily. "I used my brains, son, unlike some I could mention. No point in us both getting caught, was there?

I've been biding my time, waiting for the moment." His beady black eyes inspected Doreen. "Aren't you going to introduce me to your friend?"

"Doreen, meet Crabbit," muttered Jack.

"Pleased to meet you, princess," said Crabbit, putting his black head on one side and giving a little wink.

"Oh, Jack!" said Doreen, "You didn't say you had a talking bird! He's sweet."

"He's not," said Jack. "Believe me. There hasn't been a single moment on this adventure when he's come in useful . . ."

Behind them, the bed creaked and Eugenia gave a sudden snort. Everybody froze. Several seconds passed very slowly indeed - and then, to universal relief, the snores resumed.

"Not come in useful, eh?" muttered Crabbit sniffily. "Watch this, then!"

There was a flapping noise and a sudden release of pressure from Jake's shoulder area. Moments later, there came the sound of scrabbling from the top of the wardobe. Suddenly, a vast, wobbling shape appeared on the edge.

Jack and Doreen only just had time to jump to either side before the mighty ball of elastic came hurtling down, landing between them and bouncing once before rolling a short way over the carpet and finally coming to rest in the sea of broken glass beneath the window.

"So what do you say to that, then?" asked Crabbit triumphantly, fluttering down to join them.

"Brilliant! Wonderful! Thanks!" said Doreen, clapping her hands.

"Mmmf," said Jack.

CHAPTER FIFTEEN

THE DESCENT

In which Our Hero comes down in the world

"One more time," gasped Jack, pausing to wipe his streaming brow. "Ready - steady - heeeeeave!"

He placed his shoulder to the giant ball and pushed with all his might, grunting with exertion. It wobbled another couple of feet up the ramp.

"Once more," panted Doreen. "One more heave and we're there. Push!"

The makeshift ramp consisted of a broken chair leg which had been dragged across the floor to the window, then manhandled upright until it rested on the sill. The slope was steep, slippery and perilously narrow. Doreen and Crabbit were in front, pulling, and Jack was a few feet below, pushing. The ball of elastic was balanced precariously between them, wobbling like crazy and threatening to fall off the side any minute. If it did, it would be sure to take them with it.

"I'm losing my footing," groaned Jack, feet scrabbling wildly for purchase on the polished wood as the weight of the ball bore down on him. "I'm sliding back - I can't hold it - I . . ."

Suddenly, miraculously, the pressure lifted, and the giant ball rolled sluggishly up and onto the window ledge. Doreen reached forward and grabbed a handful of shirt as he teetered backwards, arms windmilling.

Jack found himself being jerked up and forwards, landing heavily on his knees amidst the shards of broken glass which littered the windowsill.

"Oh boy," was all he could say. "Ohboyohboyohboy."

"Are you all right?" said Doreen.

"'Course he's all right," said Crabbit. "Come on, son, pull yourself together. No time to lose. There's a nail sticking out over here, look."

There would be, thought Jack. He couldn't help feeling a bit miffed that Doreen's plan was working out so beautifully, particularly as he didn't have one. He had the niggling feeling that, so far, he hadn't contributed much to this adventure. Heroic acts had been thin on the ground, unless you counted the bending of the cage bars - and even that had been thanks to Old Mother Skinnard's surprisingly effective Extra Strength Pill.

"Right," said Doreen, briskly. "Now, I'm going to tie this end of the elastic to this extremely useful nail, using a special knot. It's one we circus folk use for the flying trapeze, so there's no chance of it slipping."

Efficiently, she began to secure the trailing end of the ball of elastic to the stout nail which so handily projected from the window frame.

As she busied herself, Jack crawled - very slowly - around the splinters of glass, through the empty window frame and onto the outer ledge. A cool night breeze soothed his fevered brow. Cautiously, he inched his way to the edge and peered down.

Far, far below, much farther than he cared to think about, light spilled from the window of a lower room out into the courtyard. Moonlight glistened on the surface of the distant pond in which lay the half submerged, buckled remains of Eugenia's doll's pram. His mouth went dry, his head swam, and he gave a little whimper.

"Oh boy," he said again.

"There," said Doreen from behind him. "That should hold. The next part's quite simple. We just push the elastic over, and it should unwind under its own weight, see? Crabbit can fly down and check where it ends. Come on, what are you doing? There's no time to lose."

Unwillingly, Jack climbed to his feet. His legs felt like jelly as he walked over to the huge ball of elastic and once again positioned himself behind it.

"Right," said Doreen. "After three. One - two - three! There she goes!"

Slowly, the giant ball rolled forward, wobbled for a moment on the edge, then plopped over, unravelling as it fell. At the same time, Crabbit launched himself off the windowsill and swooped down after it.

Jack closed his eyes and backed away from the edge, feeling giddy. When he opened them again, Crabbit was back, crouched on the windowsill with the end of the elastic dangling from his beak.

"Not quite long enough," he announced. "It stops at the kitchen windowsill. But there's a drainpipe running down next to it. You can slide down that easily enough."

"Good. Come here, Jack, and raise your arms. You're going first."

"No I'm not," said Jack, staying where he was and keeping his arms firmly by his sides.

"You've got to. You don't know how to tie yourself on properly."

"I don't care. I'm not going first."

"Oh, all right, then!" snorted Doreen, exasperated. "I'll tie us both on. We'll jump together, in tandem. How's that?"

"But the elastic'll break!"

"It won't."

"The knot'll come undone!"

"It *won't*. I know what I'm doing. Come on, quickly, quickly."

With a sinking heart, he raised his arms while Doreen passed the elastic around both their waists. She had a bit of trouble passing it through the safety pin that held her dress on but finally it was done. They stood, face to face, firmly knotted together.

"I don't want to do this," announced Jack. "I've never told anyone, but I'm height sick. Don't make me do this, Doreen."

"Sorry, can't be helped. Shuffle sideways to the edge."

They shuffled sideways to the edge. Jack turned his head away and closed his eyes.

"Right," said Doreen. "Hang on tight. I'll say 'ready, steady, go', then we jump, right? Ready . . ."

"By the way," said Crabbit.

"Steady . . ."

"Before you go . . ."

"Go!"

"Just one little thing I forgot to mention."

"Jump!"

And they jumped. Jack's stomach tried to

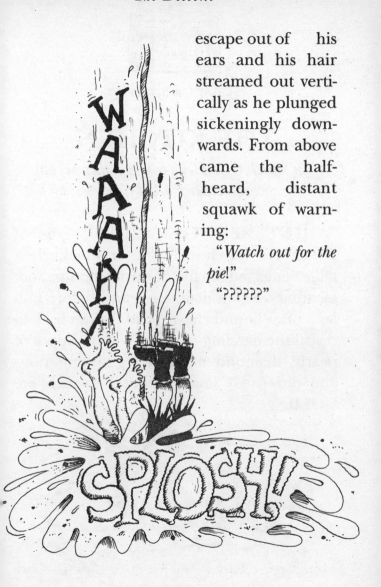

escape out of his ears and his hair streamed out vertically as he plunged sickeningly downwards. From above came the half-heard, distant squawk of warning:

"*Watch out for the pie!*"

"??????"

CHAPTER SIXTEEN

THE KITCHEN

In which Our Hero comes comes across something a bit fishy

"WHEN'S ME SUPPER READY?" growled Ebner. He was hunched over the kitchen table, engaged in his favourite occupation: gloating over his ill-gotten gains. Before him lay a brass bound chest, its lid thrown back to reveal the dazzling contents within. Ropes of pearls, diamond necklaces, glittering rings and dozens of small, canvas bags marked: **GOLD**.

He had removed his uncomfortable Smart-Giant-Going-Out-To-Lunch clothes and was now clad in Slobby-Giant-At-Home-For-The-Evening attire. This consisted of laced-up tarpaulin (what else?) shabby breeches and a pair of enormous thonged sandals.

"WHAT?" snapped Edna, through tight lips. She was busily banging cupboard doors, taking out huge plates and oversized cutlery. She wore rubber gloves, a huge starched white apron and a bitter expression.

The kitchen was a modern one, by giant standards. The surfaces gleamed. There were proper cupboards to put things in and a vast black range with brass saucepans sitting on the top. There was a deep sink with a stainless steel draining board over by the window. There were plaques hanging on the walls, saying things like *Monstrous Hands Make Light Work* and *Castle, Sweet Castle*.

"I ASKED WHEN ME SUPPER'S READY."

"I'VE COOKED THE PIE. IT'S COOLING OFF A BIT ON THE WINDOWSILL. IT WOULD HAVE BEEN READY SOONER IF WE HADN'T HAD ALL THAT FUSS AND CARRY ON WITH YOUR DAUGHTER."

"OH, I SEE!" said Ebner with a scowl. "SO SHE'S *MY* DAUGHTER NOW, IS SHE?"

"WELL, SHE'S CERTAINLY GOT YOUR TEMPER, EBNER. ALL THAT THROWING THINGS AROUND. IT CERTAINLY DOES-N'T COME FROM MY SIDE OF THE FAMI-LY."

With a little sniff, Edna yanked open a cupboard door, reached in and took out a large tin. The label read: **Mega Meaty Chunks - a Mighty Meal for Monster Moggies!**

"HERE, KITTY KITTY!" she trumpeted. "COME ON, TITANICUS, COME AND GET YOUR SUPPER."

There was an answering thump, and after a moment or two the door squeaked open. Into the kitchen, tail erect, strolled a monstrous ginger cat. It was built like a furry barrel and had baleful yellow eyes. It fixed Ebner with a steady look of cold dislike, then sauntered up to Edna and rubbed around her legs, purring.

"I SEE THE CAT GETS ITS SUPPER ON TIME," muttered Ebner.

"CERTAINLY HE DOES," snapped Edna, busy with the tin-opener. "AND THERE'S

NO POINT COMPLAINING, EBNER. IF YOU WANT YOUR SUPPER, YOU'D BETTER GET THAT TABLE CLEARED. YOU'RE AS USELESS AS YOUR SISTER, AND THAT'S SAYING SOMETHING. I SEE YOU'VE BOUGHT THAT CHEAP CAT FOOD AGAIN. YOU CAN'T EVEN GET THE SHOPPING RIGHT."

She slammed down a whacking great dish on which was piled a mountain of grey chunks sitting in a lake of cold gravy. The enormous cat stopped p u r r i n g and gave it the sort of look usually reserved for some-  thing found squashed on the side of the road.

"FUSSY, SAME AS THE REST OF THE FAMILY," muttered Ebner. "GET ALONG WITH YOU, YOU BLINKIN' ANIMAL."

"THAT'S RIGHT, TAKE IT OUT ON THE CAT. YOU CAN'T BLAME HIM. HE

SMELLS THE PIE, DON'T YOU, TITANI-CUS? YOU SMELL MUMMY'S LOVELY, LOVELY FISH PIE. EAT YOUR MEATY CHUNKS, THERE'S A GOOD PUSSY."

Titanicus gave a sneer. Then, slowly and deliberately, every hair bristling with disdain, he backed away from his dish and stalked from the room.

"IS THAT WHAT WE'RE HAVIN'? FISH PIE? WHAT KIND OF PONCY FOOD IS THAT FOR A GIANT? I HATE FISH PIE. I WANT A BUFFALO BURGER," declared Ebner sulkily.

"OH, YOU DO, DO YOU?" cried his wife. "WELL, IN THAT CASE, PERHAPS YOU'D LIKE TO COOK IT YOURSELF, INSTEAD OF SITTING AROUND PLAYING WITH YOUR TREASURE ALL NIGHT. AND I THOUGHT I TOLD YOU TO CLEAR THAT TABLE."

It all got too much for Ebner. With a roar of rage, he seized hold of the chest and up-ended it. Bags of gold came plummeting down as the glittering cascade spilled all over the floor.

"THERE!" he roared. "CLEARED! ALL

RIGHT?"

Both giants watched tiny rings, coronets and gold coins rolling away into far corners. There was a short silence.

"I SUPPOSE THAT MADE YOU FEEL BETTER?" Edna enquired in clipped tones.

"YES," growled Ebner. "IT DID."

But he did sound a bit sheepish.

"WELL, I JUST HOPE YOU'RE SATIS-FIED," said Edna. "WE CAN CERTAINLY SEE WHERE EUGENIA'S NASTY TEMPER COMES FROM NOW, CAN'T WE? THROW-ING YOUR TREASURE ALL OVER THE FLOOR LIKE A GREAT, SPOILT CHILD."

"'S' MY TREASURE," mumbled Ebner. "I NICKED IT FROM THE TITCHES. I CAN THROW IT ON THE FLOOR IF I WANT TO. YOU SHOULDN'T HAVE STOPPED ME PLAYIN' WITH IT. GIANTS ARE SUP-POSED TO PLAY WITH THEIR TREASURE. IT'S TRADITIONAL. IT'S RELAXIN'. I DESERVE A BIT OF RELAXATION AFTER WHAT I'VE PUT UP WITH TOD—"

He broke off. A distant, horribly familiar wailing sound was coming from somewhere beyond the kitchen door.

"OH, NO!" wailed Edna. "NOT AGAIN! I ONLY GOT HIM OFF HALF AN HOUR AGO!"

"WHAT'S WRONG WITH THE LITTLE PERISHER NOW?" rumbled Ebner.

"HE WANTS HIS BOTTLE, WHAT DO YOU THINK? HE WAS TOO UPSET TO HAVE IT EARLIER. OH, THUMPING THUNDERBOLTS! DO I HAVE TO THINK OF EVERYTHING? DON'T JUST SIT THERE, EBNER. HEAT HIS MILK UP. ALL RIGHT, MAXWELL, MUMMY'S COMING!"

So saying, she hurried from the room. Ebner sighed, stomped across to the cooker and started crashing about with the saucepans.

Outside, on the window ledge, Edna's enormous fish pie stood steaming gently in the cold night air. There was a ragged hole in the very centre of the crust. A length of fishy looking elastic swayed gently just above it. There was the sound of muffled sploshings and tiny voices coming from somewhere deep inside.

After a moment, the pastry gave a heave and a small, fish-coated hand rose up through the hole and gripped the edge, followed by another. Then a grey, weary figure in a fish-slimed blue dress heaved herself up and slid down the sloping crust onto the windowsill, where she stood gently dripping, sucking in great lungfuls of fresh air.

"Sorry," said Crabbit apologetically, fluttering down and landing next to her. "Tried to warn you. Too late."

"You can say that again. Look at me! Up to my armpits in fish!" Disgustedly, she began scraping handfuls of thick grey goo from herself. "Where's Jack?"

"Here," said a tired voice, and an equally fishy figure dropped down beside her. "This beats all, doesn't it?"

"It'll make a great story, though," said Crabbit hopefully.

"So it will, so it will," cried Jack heartily. "Hey! I can add it to my list! Gungee Jumping Into Fish Pie. Let me see." He ticked them off on his fingers. "That's Squashed, Dropped From A Great Height, Chased, Poked With A Hairgrip . . ."

Suddenly, he broke off. He was staring in through the open window. The kitchen was empty. From somewhere in the castle, distant, booming voices were squabbling about the correct temperature of milk.

"Wow," he said, in an awed voice. "Look at that. And they were making out they didn't have a penny left."

"What? Let's go, while the coast is clear. There's a drainpipe here, we can . . ."

"But, look." He pointed. "Look what's on the floor."

"So? It's only treasure . . ."

She broke off. She stared at him.

"No," she said. "You're crazy."

"It's what I came for," said Jack. "After all I've been through, I'll be blowed if I'm going to come away empty-handed."

"You're not going in there. It's too risky. You'll get us all caught . . ."

But she was talking to fresh air. Jack had already gone.

CHAPTER SEVENTEEN

THE CAT

In which Our Hero helps himself - with dire consequences

Titanicus the two ton cat sat outside the kitchen door, scatching at his fleas. He had all the usual cat habits - but in his case, they were magnified. He sharpened his vast claws on chairs, deposited mighty hairs all over sofas and frequently left large piles of vomit where the giants would step in them. Also, he prided himself on being an exceedingly faddy eater. Now, if you were talking crab sticks or choice prawns or a drop of double cream, that was just fine and dandy. Those he would hoover up in seconds. But when it came to your cheap and nasty common-or-garden cat food - well, that was a very different kettle of fish (or tin of grey lumps, as was usually the case.)

Titanicus had devised a simple stratagem

to deal with bad food days. He took great care never, ever to let his owners catch him in the act of eating it. His reasoning was that if they saw you actually consume the filthy stuff, they might assume you liked it and think it was all right for them to go out and buy some more.

The trick was to register one's protest with a great, theatrical walk-out the second they set down the dish, then wait until everyone was well out of the way before secretly sneaking back, usually in the dead of night, to wolf it down. Of course, this meant his dish was empty in the morning, but he hoped they would think it was mice.

Titanicus was particularly ravenous this evening. The family had been out to lunch and nobody had thought to leave him anything. When they had returned, there had been a lot of shouting and roaring which had lasted well into the evening - and when, finally, supper had arrived, it had been the dreaded Mega Meaty Chunks, which he had refused to eat on principle.

He was, however, *desperate*. Not a morsel had passed his lips since breakfast and his stomach was rattling. The Pigtailed Stamper was finally sleeping. She Who Cooks and He Who Sits had both vanished to deal with the Pink Tail-Pulling Fiend who lived in the cot upstairs. The coast was clear. Now was the time to grab a quick bite. Not too much, or else they might notice. Just a furtive mouthful or two, to tide him over.

Trying to look casual, he padded towards the kitchen door and squeezed through the gap. He was about to head for his dish, when something caught his eye. He froze on the spot. Slowly, his tail twitched from side to side. There was something coming down the tea towel. Something small. With legs.

Titanicus sank into a crouch. His fascinated yellow eyes never left the tiny creature as it dropped to the floor and began to move quickly across the floor, making a bee-line for the gleaming mess of strewn treasure.

Much to his surprise, nothing in his adventures having proved simple thus far, Jack had found getting down to floor-level quite easy. It helped that there was a sink unit standing just below the window. He had shinned down the tap and carefully edged his way along to the stainless steel draining board. Dodging the soap dish, he scurried along the grooved surface in his slippery, fish-coated boots. It was rather like trying to run on a skating rink, but he made it to the end without any serious mishap.

As luck would have it, a large hook protruded from the wall at the end of the drainer, with a monster red and white checked tea towel hanging from it. Ebner had probably used it last, because it had been carelessly put back, with the bottom edge trailing on the floor.

Jack leaned over, grabbed two handfuls of cloth, and quickly began to lower himself down.

When he reached the halfway mark, he let go and slithered the rest of the way. The second his feet touched the ground he was off, running across the vast, tiled floor towards the glittering heap at the foot of the table.

From a distance, it looked impressive. Up close, it took your breath away. Crowns, crystal goblets, ruby rings, coral bracelets, gold cuff links, tangled necklaces set with precious stones - and bag after bag of stolen gold. It was clear that Ebner had been busy.

Behind him, the tea towel began to shake. Doreen was climbing down, muttering under her breath as she did so.

"Phew! Some hoard!" remarked Crabbit, fluttering up. For once, he sounded impressed. "So. What are we going for?"

"The gold," said Jack firmly, seizing a bag and swinging it over his shoulder. From within came the satisfying clink of gold coins. "Ma said to go for the obvious."

"Them necklaces are nice," remarked Crabbit, eyes gleaming. He obviously had the traditional crow's love of shiny things. "And that diamond brooch. And what about that sapphire ring?"

"Forget it. We can't carry any more. We'll just take the one bag and leave it at tha. . ."

A sudden, urgent shriek cut him off.

"Jack! Watch out! Behind you!"

He whirled round and went pale with shock. For there, within inches of his nose, was a vast, hairy paw. And resting on that paw was a mighty chin. His unwilling eyes travelled on up the monstrous, shaggy head, taking in the squashed nose, the endlessly long whiskers and, finally - the eyes. Two hard, yellow moons. Fixed on him.

A low, menacing rumble, like the onset of thunder, came deep from within the huge creature's throat and slowly, purposefully, it raised its paw. The huge, pink, fleshy pad, claws extended like a row of scimitars, hovered directly above Jack's head.

With a hoarse croak, Crabbit launched himself into the air and flapped wildly around Titanicus's head. The giant cat took no more notice than it would of a fly. Its yellow eyes never left Jack for a second. The colossal paw remained suspended.

"Run!" Crabbit squawked down at him. He had hold of the end of one of Titanicus's whiskers, and was tugging for all he was worth. "Run, lad! Run!"

But Jack couldn't run. His legs simply refused to move. It was as though he was mesmerized. Then - suddenly - Doreen was by his side. She was screaming something, but he couldn't make out what.

She reached out and he found himself being roughly shoved to one side. He staggered, lost his balance and fell full length on his back. Some sixth sense came into play, and he rolled sideways.

WHUMPH!

The mighty paw came smashing down.

It missed, but only by a hair's breadth. And he wasn't out of trouble yet. Far from it. As he lay, winded, trying to get his breath, the yellow eyes rolled in their sockets and fixed on him once more. The massive head lowered towards him. The mouth opened, exposing two rows of spikey teeth and a lolling red tongue . . .

Doreen was still screaming at him. He shook his head groggily.

"What?" he croaked stupidly.

"The potion! Use the Love Potion! In your pocket!"

"The—? Oh. Right." The penny finally dropped. "Yes. I - er - I've got it here somewhere . . ."

The slavering mouth was now right above him. He could see the tonsils! A hot hurricane of air blasted down on him as he fumbled frantically.

His trembling fingers closed on the bottle. He pulled it out, removed the cork and with all his strength, threw it into the cavernous mouth. The tiny bottle glanced off a canine, rebounded against a molar, then vanished into the red pit at the back.

Titanicus blinked in surprise. His jaws snapped shut. He drew back. He coughed, just once. He hiccoughed. Twice.

Then, very, very slowly, like a battleship foundering, he rolled over on his back and paddled his paws in the air. From the region of his chest, there came a deep, contented rattle.

He was purring!

"Well," said Jack, sitting up and staring in amazement. "Will you look at that! He's gone all soppy."

Doreen reached out and tickled Titanicus beneath his enormous chin. He wriggled with kittenish pleasure and tried to lick her with his vast red tongue.

"Puddy puddy puddy," cooed Doreen. "Nice puddy-tat. Oooh, he likes a fuss. Look, Jack. He loves us."

"Brrr," said Crabbit, keeping a safe distance. "How can she *do* that?"

Just then, the floor began to shake. Booming voices were approaching.

"Oh no!" said Jack. "Here we go again."

He rummaged deep in his pocket, brought out the crumpled paper bag and began to undo his bootlaces.

"What are you *doing?*" wailed Doreen, her eyes on the kitchen door.

"What d'you think? Taking my boots off."

"Taking your b . . . why?"

"Because," said Jack, "the time has come to try out the Seven League Socks."

CHAPTER EIGHTEEN

THE ESCAPE

In which Our Hero gets socked

"I DON'T GET IT," growled Ebner, stomping down the stairs. "WHAT YOU GOT TO BRING HIM DOWN AGAIN FOR? HE SHOULD STAY IN HIS COT IN A PROPER MANNER. ROUTINE, THAT'S WHAT BABIES NEED."

"OH YES?" sniffed Edna, clumping down behind. Maxwell was in her arms, sucking manically on a huge bottle. "AND WHAT DO YOU KNOW ABOUT IT, EBNER? WHEN DID YOU LAST CHANGE A NAPPY? HE NEEDS HIS MUMMY. HE'S STILL UPSET, AREN'T YOU, DARLING?"

A huge pigtailed figure swathed in a pink dressing gown suddenly appeared above them.

"WHAT'S GOING ON?" demanded Eugenia, from over the banisters. She was rubbing her eyes and yawning. "WHAT'S ALL THE FUSS ABOUT?"

"OH, GREAT," said Ebner, disgusted. "NOW THE OTHER ONE'S UP. THAT'S ALL WE NEED."

"SSSSH, DARLING," said Edna. "GO BACK TO BED, THERE'S A GOOD GIRL. MAXWELL'S JUST A BIT UPSET, THAT'S ALL."

"I'M UPSET," said Eugenia. "I'M MORE UPSETTER THAN HE IS. I WANT TO COME DOWN TOO."

"WELL, YOU CAN'T," snarled Ebner. He stood in the hall, arms folded, firmly blocking the door to the kitchen. "I'VE HAD ENOUGH OF YOU FOR ONE DAY, MY GIRL. I'M GONNA EAT ME PIE IN PEACE. GET BACK IN YOUR ROOM."

"I DON'T WANT TO," whined Eugenia. "IT'S COLD UP THERE. THE WINDOW'S BROKEN."

"AND WHOSE FAULT'S THAT?" enquired her father crossly. "IF YOU WEREN'T SUCH A LITTLE VANDAL, IT WOULDN'T BE BROKEN, WOULD IT?"

"THAT'S RIPE, COMING FROM YOU,

EBNER," butted in Edna. "WHO THREW THE TREASURE ALL OVER THE FLOOR IN A TEMPER, I'D LIKE TO KNOW?"

She removed the empty bottle from Maxwell's mouth and heaved him onto her shoulder, where he was violently sick.

"BRRRRRR," moaned Eugenia, collapsing onto a stair and shivering theatrically. "BRRRRRR. I'M COLD, MA. AN' I'M HUNGRY. I WANT SOME PIE. I CAN COME DOWN FOR A BIT, CAN'T I, MA?"

"WELL - ALL RIGHT, DARLING, BUT ONLY FOR A LITTLE WHILE," conceded Edna tiredly. "JUST UNTIL YOU'RE WARMED UP. AND ONLY A SPOONFUL OF PIE, MIND."

"I DON'T BELIEVE THIS!" exploded Ebner. "ISN'T A GIANT MASTER IN HIS OWN HOUSE? FLIPPIN' KIDS! WHO'D HAVE 'EM?"

So saying, he wrenched open the kitchen door. And stopped, eyes bulging in shock at the scene which met his eyes.

The cat was stretched out full length on the floor, purring and drooling, claws working in and out, yellow eyes misty with love.

And before him, scurrying around frantically inches from his nose, were . . .

"SQUEAKY!" shrieked Eugenia, ducking under Ebner's elbow. "PRINCESS TINKLE-BELL!"

She started forward, tripped over her dressing gown and crashed to the floor, like a felled oak.

"MY GOLD!" roared Ebner. "TITCHIES ARE NICKING MY GOLD!"

"WHAT?" wailed Edna.

"BLURK!" sicked-up Maxwell, not to be outdone.

"QUICK!" howled Eugenia, struggling to her knees. "THROW A TOWEL OVER THEM! DON'T LET THEM ESCAPE, PA!"

"I WON'T," hollered Ebner. "DON'T YOU WORRY ABOUT THAT!"

And he strode into the room and lifted his huge, sandaled foot, ready to stamp down with all his might.

"NO!" screamed Eugenia. "DON'T SQUASH SQUEAKY! DON'T TRAMPLE TINKLEBELL! NOOOOOOOOO!"

She needn't have worried. She had an unexpected ally.

Titanicus, you see, was in love. His new, sweet, dear, adored little playmates, the ones he loved even more - and he never thought he'd say this - even more than his catnip mouse, were about to be ground underfoot before his very eyes! With a furious yowl, he launched himself into the air - and a split second later, Ebner received a faceful of spitting, snarling, fur-wrapped venom.

Far below, Jack stood in his socks, arms clasped firmly around a bag of gold. There was no time to put his boots back on. Doreen clung on to his back like a monkey, her arms encircling his neck. Over their heads, Crabbit flapped to and fro, shrieking at them to hurry.

"Right," said Jack grimly. "This is it, Doreen. Hang on tight and hope for the best. Here we go!"

He took a tentative step - and soared!

It was wonderful. It was like flying. Up, up he rose, as effortlessly as a tuft of thistledown, up and forward in a graceful arc, covering half the distance between the table and the distant open window in a single bound.

"Wheeee!" shrieked Doreen in his ear.

"Geronimo!" squawked Crabbit, flapping alongside. "That's the way to do it, son!"

Then they were sinking. Down, down they sailed, the floor rising to meet them. One foot lightly touched the surface, then they were rising again in another great, curving jump, higher this time, up and over the sink . . .

"SHUT THE WINDOW! THEY'RE ESCAPING!"

"GET OFF, YOU BLINKIN' ANIMAL!"

"WHAT?"

"STOP!"

"BLURRRRK!"

Pandemonium reigned. Eugenia finally regained her feet, stepped on a rope of pearls and lurched into Ebner, who was staggering blindly around with his eyes full of cat. Edna simply stood stock still, saying "WHAT?" and clutching hold of Maxwell, who enthusiastically continued to vomit down her back.

Balletically, Jack landed lightly on the window ledge, took off yet again . . .

And they were through! Out through the window they sailed, over the stone-cold pie with the gaping hole in the middle, over the pond with the puzzled goldfish swimming around the remains of Eugenia's pram, then slowly, gracefully, down into the courtyard for another brief touchdown before rising up

again, up and over the wrought iron gate into
a world of cloud, silver moonlight, white road
and blissful, blissful silence.

CHAPTER NINETEEN

THE PARTING

*In which Our Hero takes leave of an old
friend*

"I can't believe you're doing this," said
Doreen.

"Got to. Can't leave without saying goodbye."

They stood on the top step of the
giantess's castle, staring up at the vast oaken
door. A cold night wind blew a few stray
leaves across the shadowy courtyard below.
To one side of them swung the bell rope.
From within, the echoes of distant clanging
died away.

"Why?" asked Doreen.

Jack thought about this. He thought
about the giantess, eating her way through a
ton of chocolate in order to push away the
loneliness.

And whose fault was it that she was lonely? His.

He thought about her shabby clothes and the way the castle was falling down around her ears.

Whose fault was it that she was poor? His.

He thought about the bacon sandwiches, the interesting conversations they had had and the way she had always tried to protect him. He thought of the shy way she had confessed that she had a soft spot for titchies. He thought about her determination to make the best of things.

He thought all of this. And he said: "Because, once I did a terrible thing. And I'm sorry. And anyway, it's only polite."

"Huh!" said Doreen.

Shivering, Jack hopped from one frozen foot to the other. The Seven League Socks had proved wonderfully efficient in the Quick Means Of Escape department, but warm they were not.

With the aid of the socks, they had quickly covered the journey back to the castle in a series of immense, soaring leaps. Each incredible bound had taken them further along the white gravel road, so high that they could almost see over the heaped banks of moonlit clouds that billowed on either side. It had seemed no time at all before the giantess's crumbling pile reared up ahead of them.

They could have passed on by, of course - but they didn't, because this was when Jack had made his decision. To Doreen's surprise, he had suddenly veered sharp left and with one final bound, they had soared through the archway and across the entire length of the courtyard, landing neatly on the top step, where Jack had set down the bag of gold and heaved on the bell rope with all his might.

"You're being ridiculous," protested Doreen as they waited. "We've just got away from one lot of giants and now you're voluntarily coming to call on another. It's like escaping from the lion's den and then popping in to see the bear. Don't you think so, Crabbit?"

Silence.

"Crabbit?" She stared around. "Jack, where's Crabbit?"

"Haven't a clue," said Jack with a shrug.

"But he was here a minute ago. He was flying just above us. Perhaps he's gone to the beanstalk. We should go too. Come on. Stop being so stubborn." She tugged at his arm. "It won't take us any time with those socks of yours."

"Ah," said Jack, heavily. "Ah. Doreen, there's one small thing I think I should tell you. There - um- isn't a beanstalk."

Doreen stared at him with horrified eyes.

"*What?* You were *lying?*"

"Oh no, no. There *was* one. I climbed up it. But it's gone. All there is now is a gaping great hole in the clouds. I suspect snails. And another thing . . ."

"Don't tell me," begged Doreen. "I can't take any more bad news."

"Another thing," went on Jack relentlessly. "We can't rely on the socks any more. Old Mother Skinnard told me they could only be used once. Now we've stopped, they seem to have run out of steam. Look." He waved a foot in the air and flapped his arms ineffectually. "See?"

"Well, that's just terrific," snorted Doreen. "What on earth did you stop for? Of all the stupid, idiotic, brainless—"

She broke off. From behind the door came the sound of heavy, shuffling footsteps, followed by the rattling of chains. Then, slowly, the great door swung open and for the second time, Jack found himself staring at a vast, familiar pair of carpet slippers.

"WELL, WELL, WELL," boomed the giantess. "YOU AGAIN. FUNNY TIME OF NIGHT TO COME CALLING."

178

This time, she was wearing an enormous, faded old dressing gown and her hair was in curlers.

"I've come to say goodbye," said Jack.

"HAVE YOU NOW? GOT AWAY FROM EUGENIA, THEN?"

"Oh, yes. With a bit of help from my friends."

"HMM. THOUGHT YOU MIGHT. REGULAR LITTLE ESCAPE ARTIST, AREN'T WE?"

"You know me," said Jack, modestly. From behind him, Doreen made a disgusted noise.

"AS A MATTER OF FACT, I WAS THINKING ABOUT YOU. I WAS GOING TO STROLL OVER TO EBNER'S TOMORROW, JUST TO CHECK YOU WERE ALL RIGHT. BUT I CAN SEE YOU ARE, SO YOU'VE SAVED ME THE TROUBLE."

She broke off, wrinkled her nose and sniffed mightily.

"WHAT'S THAT FISHY SMELL?" she enquired.

"Us," Jack told her. Adding, "It's a long story. I'd tell you all about it, but I suppose we ought to be getting along."

"OH WELL, SUIT YOURSELF. I DON'T SUPPOSE YOU'LL BE COMING UP THIS WAY AGAIN?"

"No. I'm pretty sure that this will be my last time."

"WELL, IF YOU DO, CALL IN. ALWAYS PLEASED TO SEE YOU."

"Thanks. Oh, and one last thing . . ." To Doreen's amazement, he picked up the bag of gold that lay at his feet and held it out. "This is for you. It's not much, and I know it doesn't make up for everything, but I just wanted to say thank you. Buy yourself some chocolate or something. I - er - shouldn't mention it to Ebner."

The giantess looked quite touched. With an effort, she bent down and gently took the bag from him.

"WELL, THANKS," she said. "VERY THOUGHTFUL, I'M SURE. YOU'RE A GOOD LITTLE TEA LEAF. FOR A TITCHY."

Then she straightened, turned and quietly went back into her castle, shutting the door behind her.

"Don't say anything," said Jack to Doreen, who was staring at him in astonishment. "Just don't, all right?"

Tiredly, he began to lower himself down the steps. When he got to the bottom, he hobbled off across the courtyard, wincing as he went, not even looking back to see where Doreen had got to.

As Jack limped through the arch, Doreen caught him up.

"I just wanted to say one thing," she said, linking her arm with his.

"What?"

"That was very sweet, what you just did. In fact, it was the sweetest, kindest, bravest, most generous thing I've ever seen."

"Really?" said Jack, surprised. He wasn't used to compliments these days. "Well - er - thanks. I'm not sure Ma will see it that way, though," he added with a sigh.

"Well, I do," said Doreen stoutly. "Come on."

"Where to?"

"To the end of the road. That's where the hole in the clouds is, isn't it?"

"Well, yes, but - there's nothing there. Except the hole."

"That's a start, isn't it? You never know -

maybe another beanstalk will have grown overnight or something," said Doreen hopefully.

But one hadn't.

Some time later, they stood staring down into the cloud fringed, black, empty pit which plunged down into misty nothingness.

"Oh well," sighed Jack. "That's that, then."

He flopped down and rubbed his sore feet. The long walk back along the gravel road had taken a severe toll. There was nothing left of the Seven League Socks except a few shreds of ragged wool flapping around his ankles.

"It isn't!" shouted Doreen fiercely. "It can't be! There's got to be a way. What else have you got in your pocket?"

"Nothing," said Jack, with a tired little shrug. "We've used up all the stuff Old Mother Skinnard gave me. There isn't a handy hot air balloon or flying carpet, if that's what you . . . what's that noise?"

There was a distant rumbling. The millions of little stones that made up the white road were vibrating in an all-too-familiar way.

"Is that what I think it is?" Doreen clutched his arm.

"Yep," said Jack grimly. "'Fraid so. It's the coach."

They looked back along the white road. Yes, it was coming. They could see it in the distance. It had already passed the giantess's castle and was hurtling madly towards them. Moonlight glinted on the windows and great fountains of stones sprayed out on either side, kicked up by immense hooves. From within came the sound of distant howling.

"Well," said Doreen, grimly. "We can't stay here and be captured again. There's only one thing for it. We have to jump."

"*Jump*? Are you *mad*? Have you any idea how far down it is?"

"Maybe something'll break our fall . . ."

"Yes. Like the ground. Doreen, I've done some crazy things while I've been up here, but there's no way, absolutely no way that I'm going to . . ."

"Look!"

He broke off. Doreen was standing on the very edge, looking down into the black pit and pointing, eyes wide. Nervously, he edged up behind her and looked down.

There was something coming up towards them. A small, black dot, getting bigger by the second. As it rose from the depths, Jack thought there was something familiar about it. He recognised that matted grey hair and that billlowing cloak. In fact, it wasn't a some-thing, it was a somebody . . . and seated on

her shoulder was an even more familiar black shape!

"Well, now, Crabbit," said Old Mother Skinnard, rising up through the hole in the clouds and hovering before them on her broomstick. "Looks like you fetched me in the nick of time."

CHAPTER TWENTY

THE HAPPY ENDING

In which Our Hero finally becomes just that

"So," Jack summed up, for the admiring village children clustered at his feet. "That's: Squashed, Chased, Poked With A Hairgrip, Stuck-up With Toffee Papers, Imprisoned In A Bird Cage, Gungee Jumping Into Fish Pie, Attacked By A Giant Cat, Pursued Whilst Wearing Seven League Socks then Rescued At The Eleventh Hour By A Genuine Witch On A Broomstick. Have I left anything out?"

A small boy put his hand up.

"Please, Jack. Dropped From A Great Height, Jack."

"Well spotted, Tommy Lettuce. Glad to hear you're paying attention."

"What are you doing?" asked Doreen, coming up behind. She was wearing a normal dress and her shaggy hair was neatly covered with a headscarf. She looked rather odd without the enormous safety pin sprouting from between her shoulder blades. Jack couldn't quite get used to it.

"I was just telling them the story again."

"Well, hurry it up. Your ma says everybody's up at the Snail Farm, waiting to give you a hero's send-off."

Snail Farm. That was something else Jack couldn't get used to.

Arriving back home empty-handed hadn't been as disastrous as he had thought it would be. Giant time moves much, much slower than human time, and he found that a lot had happened in his absence.

Much to his amazement, he found that his ma's circumstances had changed beyond belief. Pleased though she was to have him home again, she was too busy to make that much of a fuss of him, being involved in a new business venture which was taking up all her time.

It had happened like this. Coming out into the garden the morning after his departure, she had been dismayed to find thousands of bloated, juicy, smug looking snails crawling all over a pile of stripped sticks, which was all that remained of the beanstalk.

However, instead of throwing her apron over her head and sitting down for a good bawl, for once Jack's ma had used her brains. She had spent the morning gathering them up and packing them into containers ready to ship off to France, where they were considered a real delicacy, with an unusual bean-like flavour.

Several bulging bags stuffed with French francs had arrived by return of post, which she had immediately invested back into the business, with the result that her Snail Farm was now a thriving concern, employing the entire population of the village in the catching, fattening-up and packaging process.

So successful was the business proving that she had moved back into the palace, filling the throne room with huge packing cases, and employing a team of accountants who sat around long desks in what was once the ballroom, totting up long columns of figures which added up to vast profits.

Jack was pleased for her, of course, but somehow he couldn't see himself settling down to snail farming. He felt restless. The trouble was, he couldn't decide what to do next. Be a snail farmer? No. Be a hero? Been there, done it, never again. That's why he had been so very pleased when Doreen made her suggestion.

"Come on," she said again. "The Mayor's all ready to make his speech. It looks like there's an awful lot of it."

"Do you know, Doreen," said Jack, "I don't think I'm all that bothered about hearing the Mayor's speech. In fact, I think I'll give the whole hero's send-off a miss, if that's all right with you. I don't suppose it'll be much different from a hero's welcome home, and I've had one of those before."

"Suits me," said Doreen, with a shrug. "Let's go, then. No time like the present."

"Where you goin', Jack?" asked one of the admiring village children as he stood up.

"I," announced Jack, "am off to join the Chippolata Brothers' circus. Me and my friend here are working on a double act. We're not sure what it's going to be, but I've a feeling it might involve elastic and a barrel of gunge somewhere along the line."

"Aint you gonna kill any more giants?" asked another, sounding a bit disappointed.

"Not on your life," said Jack, with feeling. And this time, he meant it.

The sun was beginning to set as they walked off down the lane.

"So that's that, then," Jack remarked to Doreen. "Everything's ended satisfactorily. Ma's up to her neck in snails, so she doesn't need me any more, and I'm off to join a circus. I'm looking forward to the elephants. They're big, you say?"

"Not *that* big," said Doreen. "Not after what we've been used to."

"Good. Then there's only one thing that I keep wondering about."

"What's that?"

"Old Mother Skinnard. What did she hope to get out of all this? I can't believe she didn't have some ulterior motive. Oh - er - hello, Mrs Skinnard. I was just talking about you."

"I know," said Old Mother Skinnard. She was standing next to the five barred gate, inspecting a notice on a pole which she had just finished hammering into the ground. "I 'eard. You was wonderin' why I went to all that trouble on your account."

"Yes. I was, actually."

"Because you aint afraid to spend a bit of

time with lonely old ladies. That's why. One good turn deserves another. You 'elps me, I 'elps you. That's the way the world goes. Or should go. Besides . . ."

She tapped on the notice, with an air of pride. A large, painted arrow pointed in the direction of her distant hovel. Underneath were the words:

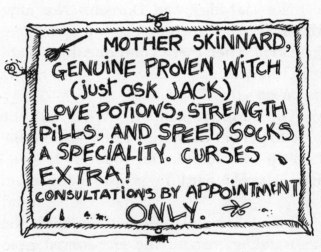

MOTHER SKINNARD,
GENUINE PROVEN WITCH
(just ask JACK)
LOVE POTIONS, STRENGTH
PILLS, AND SPEED SOCKS
A SPECIALITY. CURSES
EXTRA!
CONSULTATIONS BY APPOINTMENT
ONLY.

"Besides, I've got you to thank for an upsurge in me witch career. The word gets round, you know. I gets taken seriously now. I'm gettin' a bit of respect for once. People looks nervous when they sees me comin'."

She gave a pleased little chuckle.

"Well, well," said Jack cheerfully. "Nervous, eh? That's great."

"Oh, yes. They goes out of their way to avoid me. Kids run screamin' at the mention of me name."

"Wonderful!"

"It is. 'Course, it should 'ave 'appened years ago, but I've never been one to push meself forward. Anyway, it's all different now, oh dear me, yes. I'm a local legend now, thanks to you."

"Glad to hear it. Congratulations, Mrs Skinnard. It couldn't have happened to a nice . . . scarier woman."

"An' I'll tell you something else," continued Old Mother Skinnard, sounding smug. "I'm gettin' loads of enquiries, mostly from youngsters like yerself, wantin' to be sent off on darin' adventures with a guaranteed happy endin'. All the ones what don't want to work up at yer ma's Snail Farm. I hear she's doin' all right, by the way."

"She is," said Jack. "She's taken to business like a duck to water."

"More like a snail to a beanstalk," chortled Old Mother Skinnard. "Oh, well. At least she's doin' somethin' for 'erself. Standin' on 'er own feet. That's because she didn't 'ave you around to go blamin' all the time. So I did 'er a favour as well as you."

"I suppose you did," said Jack thoughtfully. "Thanks."

"Don't mention it. So. A little bird told me you'm off to join the circus, is that right?"

"It certainly is," said Jack. "We're thinking of a high wire act. Heights hold no fear for me any more, after all I've been through. We'll be coming back this way next spring. I'll save you a seat in the front row. Next to Ma."

"Very kind of you, I'm sure. Oh, just one thing before you go. I got somethin' for you."

She placed her fingers to her lips and gave a shrill whistle. There was a familiar whooshing noise, and suddenly, Jack found his shoulder gripped by a well known set of claws.

"Mornin', lad. Mornin', princess. Here we all are, then. The old team, eh?"

"What d'you think you're doing?" enquired Jack.

"What d'you think? Coming with you. I'm going to be a circus crow. Gonna fly through flamin' hoops. She's got herself a toad. Don't want me no more."

"And what makes you think *we* want you?"

"Oh, Jack!" Doreen leapt to Crabbit's defence. "Don't be mean. Take no notice, Crabbit, darling, of course he wants you really."

"No I don't. I don't like talking birds. I've never liked talking birds . . ."

"What kind of gratitude is that, after all I've done for you . . ."

Bickering amiably, the three of them strolled down the lane, over the hills and far away, where elephants roamed and your life was your own to do with as you liked.

AND THE GIANTS?

That's all very well, I hear you say. A nice, romantic ending with sunsets and circuses and all that. But what became of the giants? Well, perhaps we'll let them have the last word.

VIOLET: ME? OH, I'M ALL RIGHT. HAD A BIG WIN AT THE BINGO. I'M PUTTING THE CASTLE ON THE MARKET NEXT WEEK. I'VE SEEN A NICE BUNGALOW, JUST UP THE ROAD FROM MRS THUN-DERTHIGHS. IN THE MEANTIME, I'VE GOT ME CROSSWORDS AND ME CHOCO-LATES. I'M THINKIN' OF GETTING ME HAIR DONE. YES. I'M ALL RIGHT.

EBNER: TITCHIES? DON'T TALK TO ME ABOUT TITCHIES. WHY, HAVE YOU GOT ONE? WHERE'S THE MUSTARD, I'LL 'AVE IT . . .

EUGENIA: I DON'T CARE ANYWAY. TITCHIES ARE POOEY. I'M GETTING A HAMSTER, SO THERE.

EDNA: DON'T SAY THAT WORD, EUGENIA!

MAXWELL: "WAAAAAAAAAAAAAH!!"

Some things never change.

Another Hodder Children's Book

The Emperor's Gruckle Hound

Kathryn Cave

Illustrated by Chris Riddell

Sam sleeps in a palace on silk cushions and feasts on salmon.

Little does he know that his brother Scruff hides from burgled butchers and searches for slops in city bins.

What if they were to change places? Could anybody tell the difference?

A wonderful tale of twin puppies by a prize-winning team.

Another Hodder Children's Book

The Haunted Suitcase
and other stories

Colin Thompson

In a small seaside town stands a tall dark
house. Every brick from the steep chimneys
to the deepest cellar is dripping with memories
and ghosts:

The haunted suitcase is churning out every
lost sock in the world. That old sea dog,
Dogbreath Magroo, has spent centuries
spreading hairs. And the Plughole Fairy is
causing chaos in the bathroom.

This is no ordinary haunted house . . .

A hilarious collection of short stories.

Darren the Sun God

Brough Girling

Illustrated by Chris Smedley

It's thousands of years ago. Your dad hadn't even started proper school, and a sabre-toothed tiger lurks round every corner. But that's not what's bothering the mud people! Their sacred crystal has been stolen! And it's up to Rocco and Roxanna to solve the mystery.

Even facing a Sabre Tooth is better than a day in the world's first primary school!

During the Age of the Mud, *anything* can happen . . . and it does.

Fearsome Tales for Fiendish Kids

Jamie Rix

Illustrated by Ross Collins

'The needle, nurse,' said Dr Moribundus. It was five fee long, like a javelin. Lorelei Lee whimpered.

What terrible cure lies in store for the girl who feigns illness when it's time to go to school? And what about *Serena Slurp*, the greedy guzzler who can't stop gorging? Or *Johnny Bullneck*, the bully who gets his fingers burnt (and more!). And *Bessy O'Messy*, whose bedroom is like a bomb pit. Or *Well'ard Willard*, who tells his last lie - and doesn't live to regret it.

Grim and ghastly fates await fiendish kids with horrible habits.

Prepare to laugh, gasp and squirm as you read these brilliant cautionary tales.

ORDER FORM

0 340 65599 2   THE EMPEROR'S GRUCKLE HOUND   £3.5
Kathryn Cave

0 340 64849 X   THE HAUNTED SUITCASE   £3.9
Colin Thompson

0 340 63443 X   DARREN THE SUN GOD   £3.9
Brough Girling

0 340 64095 2   FEARSOME TALES FOR FIENDISH KIDS   £3.9
Colin Thompson

All Hodder Children's books are available at your local bookshop or newsagent, or can
ordered direct from the publisher. Just tick the titles you want and fill in the form below. Pri
and availability subject to change without notice.

Hodder Children's Books, Cash Sales Department, Bookpoint, 39 Milton Pa
Abingdon, OXON, OX14 4TD, UK. If you have a credit card you may order
telephone - (01235) 831700.

Please enclose a cheque or postal order made payable to Bookpoint Ltd to the val
of the cover price and allow the following for postage and packing: UK & BFP
- £1.00 for the first book, 50p for the second book, and 30p for each additior
book ordered up to a maximum charge of £3.00. OVERSEAS & EIRE - £2.
for the first book, £1.00 for the second book, and 50p for each additional boo

Name ....

Address...
....
....

If you would prefer to pay by credit card, please complete:

Please debit my Visa/ Access/ Diner's Club/ American Express (delete as applic
able) card no:

Signature ....

Expiry Date...